sex, a mystery

SEX,
a mystery

fiona quirina

BERKLEY PRIME CRIME, NEW YORK

THE BERKLEY PUBLISHING GROUP
Published by the Penguin Group
Penguin Group (USA) Inc.
375 Hudson Street, New York, New York 10014, USA
Penguin Group (Canada), 10 Alcorn Avenue, Toronto, Ontario M4V 3B2, Canada
(a division of Pearson Penguin Canada Inc.)
Penguin Books Ltd., 80 Strand, London WC2R 0RL, England
Penguin Group Ireland, 25 St. Stephen's Green, Dublin 2, Ireland (a division of Penguin Books Ltd.)
Penguin Group (Australia), 250 Camberwell Road, Camberwell, Victoria 3124, Australia
(a division of Pearson Australia Group Pty. Ltd.)
Penguin Books India Pvt. Ltd., 11 Community Centre, Panchsheel Park, New Delhi—110 017, India
Penguin Group (NZ), Cnr. Airborne and Rosedale Roads, Albany, Auckland 1310, New Zealand
(a division of Pearson New Zealand Ltd.)
Penguin Books (South Africa) (Pty.) Ltd., 24 Sturdee Avenue, Rosebank, Johannesburg 2196,
South Africa

Penguin Books Ltd., Registered Offices: 80 Strand, London WC2R 0RL, England

This book is an original publication of The Berkley Publishing Group.

This is a work of fiction. Names, characters, places, and incidents either are the product of the author's imagination or are used fictitiously, and any resemblance to actual persons, living or dead, business establishments, events, or locales is entirely coincidental.

First edition: March 2005

Library of Congress Cataloging-in-Publication Data

Quirina, Fiona.
    Sex, a mystery / Fiona Quirina.—1st ed.
        p.   cm
    ISBN 0-425-20034-5 (alk. paper)
        1. Women detectives—New York (State)—New York—Fiction. 2. New York (N.Y.)—Fiction.
        3. Prostitutes—Fiction. I. Title.

PS3617.U59S49 2005
813'.6—dc22

                                                                          2004057004

PRINTED IN THE UNITED STATES OF AMERICA

10 9 8 7 6 5 4 3 2 1

sex, a mystery

It's an old joke.

The john comes up to the call girl's apartment, and while she's fixing him his complimentary brandy, he pokes around the place. Over the bed he spots a diploma from Princeton, then another—an MA in engineering from MIT—and finally an MBA from Harvard.

"Wow! Are all those *yours*?" he asks the call girl.

"Yup."

"How the hell did you end up in this business?"

"Just lucky, I guess," the call girl says.

Well, I can't say I'm always lucky, but I do get by very nicely, thank you. These days, I have only three or four visitors a week, steady customers every one of them, more than enough to keep me and Father Paddy Riordin comfortably ensconced in our Lower Fifth Avenue duplex. Not to mention enough to keep Paddy's "Homeless Ministries" afloat. It's an elegant little economic cycle; Paddy likes to call my bedroom "Sherwood Forest."

And no, I didn't go to Princeton; I graduated from Barnard—a magna in French literature and philosophy. But I do have an MBA from Harvard, that celebrated pipeline to the executive suites of the Fortune 500. I even worked my way up to one of those suites—at a food conglomerate that shall remain nameless. My title was Senior Vice President of International Marketing, and I quickly developed a reputation for cutting-edge deals, like the time I sold several tons of frozen pork chops to an Israeli supermarket chain. That is, I enjoyed this reputation until I discovered one of our most profitable exports, baby formula, was causing wholesale malnutrition in the children of our Third World customers—sixteen-point-three million dollars' worth of malnutrition annually, to be exact.

I will spare you the details of the public stink I made about this bit of business, the so-called "Formula Fiasco." It ended up costing my employer half a billion in revenues. All it cost me was my job. Plus the various other executive positions I discovered I was suddenly unqualified to fill when I went job hunting soon after that debacle. When reflecting on the entire episode, I have to smile at how naive I was in the beginning. It's not like I hadn't paid attention in my "Business Ethics" class at Harvard; it's just that it had all seemed so charmingly theoretical back then.

Of course, that is only half the story.

The other half is how I ended up in the world's oldest profession, albeit the elite reaches of that profession. I am sorry, but I cannot offer you a tawdry story of my fall from grace into the clutches of some Svengali who turned me into a sex slave. Or of an escalating drug habit that reduced me to prostituting myself for my next fix. The only substance habit I have is champagne, preferably Veuve Clicquot, but that habit is simply an accouterment to my current lifestyle, not the cause of it. Nonetheless, this *is* a story about money. Hey, what isn't?

Frank Macy was my lover before he became my first customer. He was married, which bothered him infinitely more than it bothered me. I liked his company very much, but the idea of having a permanent consecrated relationship with Frank never appealed to me in the least. All I had to do was imagine Frank returning home to me every evening, furrow-browed and edgy after a long day on Wall Street, for me to offer up a blessing of good health and long life to his loyal wife. I guess I am just not the domestic type, at least not in the usual sense. Which is to say, unless you call keeping house with a celibate priest the usual sense. Heaven knows, to Paddy and me, our arrangement seems as normal as orange juice. It is certainly more tranquil than the Osbournes.

After the food conglomerate terminated my employment with only six months' severance pay, I went into a kind of yuppy denial: I kept my duplex, I kept my charge account at Saks Fifth Avenue, I continued to add to my collection of first editions of Baudelaire and Celine. So here and there, I began accepting temporary loans from good old Frank. I was confident that I would be able to pay him back in full, complete with interest, as soon as the dust settled on my whistle-blower episode.

But the dust never settled. After a while, even the Harvard

Business School placement office stopped returning my calls. I considered my options. Launch my own business? How about becoming a private marketing consultant? Or perhaps something entirely different, say, open a health spa in Newport? Yes, that one sounded particularly appealing. I still knew enough well-heeled types to raise the capital for such a venture. Like Frank, for example.

But Frank's reaction caught me by surprise. He was distraught at the prospect of my leaving the city. I told him he could visit me in Newport. I reminded him that *he* was married and *we* were not. But Frank said, "I like things just the way they are, Lydia."

"Me too," I said. "But we're grown-ups. We'll make the adjustment."

And that was when Frank said, "What if I, you know, contributed to your upkeep on a regular basis?"

I laughed. "You mean, like a kept woman," I said.

"I don't know," Frank responded. "Like you say, we're grown-ups. We can do what we want and call it whatever we want."

"In that case, I'd rather call myself a courtesan," I replied, winking, going for a wry laugh. But that word, "courtesan," felt astonishingly delicious on my lips. It summoned up images of the Venetian Renaissance, La Traviata, and of that marvelous portrait of a bejeweled courtesan by il Vecchio that I have lingered over so often at the Metropolitan Museum. God knows, the courtesans of seventeenth-century Venice were not only the most elegant women in town, but by far the wealthiest, most educated, and independent women in all of Europe.

One could do worse.

Like, for example, going back to work for another soulless Fortune 500 conglomerate.

So Frank became my first paying customer. And then, soon after that, along came my old friend, Dr. Sylvia Kahn, with a string of clients or patients or whatever you want to call them: Abe, Michael, and Raphael.

Just lucky, I guess.

1

Tuesdays are Michael—Michael Peabody Linscott III, a Boston Brahmin with a nose straight enough to impeccably line up columns on a bank statement. Michael is aristocratically handsome, tall, fit, rich, and given to fits of melancholy. As with the others, he first came to me as a professional referral from Sylvia, my former Barnard classmate who earns significantly more than I do as an uptown sex therapist.

Like most sex therapists', Sylvia's practice took a serious hit when Viagra arrived on the market. But her business began to recover when the small print in the Viagra pamphlet made itself known in marital bedrooms: The little blue pill works its magic only when the pill taker is turned on by his partner. Thus, many of Sylvie's male patients were back to square one: Theirs wasn't a vascular problem, it was an erotic one, and they remained dead in bed. For them, the thrill was simply gone.

Sylvie subscribes to the old Masters and Johnson thesis that Eros is a giant who dozes off from boredom, stress, and familiar routine. And like Masters and Johnson, one fix in Sylvie's playbook is a "sex surrogate." That would be me, Lydia Quess. Sylvie arranges for me to rouse the sleeping giants in men like Michael, men whose zest for sex—indeed, for all of life—has been rendered unconscious by the dreariness of their daily lives.

There is not a doubt in my mind that Renaissance courtesans would have considered themselves "sex surrogates"—or even possibly "sex therapists"—if that lingo had been around then. In Teodora di Sebastiano's marvelous diaries of her life as Venice's most sought-after courtesan, she wrote of one of her gentlemen visitors, Count di Compte (a witty pseudonym, I'm sure), who "compared me to an elixir that brings to life all that has been deadened in him by church and society. I am the cure for all that ails him." By the by, this is the same Signorina di Sebastiano who wrote in her *Letter to a Venetian Woman*, "My dear, a young lady with your qualities need never worry about finances. You are literally sitting upon your most valuable asset."

One obvious flaw in the Masters and Johnson cure is that once a surrogate rouses the sleeping giant in a man, both giant and man become deeply attached to her. A no-brainer, really. Teodora di Sebastiano knew that; in fact, she counted on it. True, Michael was capable of resuming his marital duties after a few joyful evenings in my bedroom, but the idea of giving me up seemed patently absurd to him. Sylvia made a valiant attempt to get Michael to "transfer his erotic sensitivities" entirely to his wife, but his heart wasn't in it.

As I say, he comes on Tuesdays.

Tuesday is also the afternoon and evening when Paddy ministers to the destitute under Grand Central Station. Paddy and his assistant, Manuel, park their paneled truck on Third Avenue, where they fill their backpacks with children's orange-flavored, chewable vitamin pills (the only kind their clientele will take), protein chocolate bars, beef jerky, instant coffee, and toilet paper. Needless to mention, "Homeless Ministries" is not affiliated with the New York Diocese, let alone the Church of Rome. Paddy's only affiliation, God love him, is the brotherhood of man.

Paddy's absence allows me to serve Michael a little champagne and caviar snack downstairs before we make our way up to my bedroom. Often, we put on some vintage Sinatra and dance awhile, champagne flutes in hand. Michael is a fine dancer, courtly yet graceful. Occasionally, he sings along with Frankie, *"My funny valentine, sweet funny valentine."* Whenever Michael sings, it is a sure sign the lovemaking to follow will be particularly lyrical.

Michael sang that night.

We made love leisurely, stretching it out for more than two hours with breaks for sips of champagne and some bouncy dancing in the nude on top of my bed. I loved Michael more than usual that evening; it seemed to me it was not just the sleeping giant I had awakened in him, but the sleeping Exeter boy who had never once dared to play hooky. As always, he regaled me with his regular postcoital fantasy about quitting it all and going to live in Paris with me, this time embroidering his delusion with an adorable scene of the two of us scouring the kiosks along the Seine for first editions of Rimbaud. Sweet.

Right after climax, there must be a hormone men secrete that bathes their brains with bohemian dreams. Of course, both hormone and dream evaporate the moment they pull their socks on. But this time Michael added he had a megadeal brewing that would make his dream come true any day now. He requested another bottle of champagne to toast our new lives together.

Now, I have no desire to live with anybody except Paddy— in Paris or anywhere else—at this point in my life, but there was no reason for me to mention this to Michael. Part of my service is indulging fantasies, and we had already toasted our "new lives" a half-dozen times in the past. It made him happy.

It was a little after ten when I slipped downstairs to grab that second bottle of champagne. Sinatra was still crooning on the CD player, *"Come fly with me . . ."* Naked, the fresh bottle of Veuve Clicquot my only accessory, I pranced around a bit, then popped the cork before I started back up the stairway. *"If you can use, some exotic booze, there's a bar in far Bombay—"*

The sight of Michael's body sprawled spread-eagle, facedown on my bed, brought a smile to my lips for a fraction of a second. *By God,* I thought, *my star patient is doing shtick now—the Boston Brahmin goes Comedy Central.* But then I saw the ice pick buried between his shoulder blades and the blood leaking out around it, spilling onto the sheets.

I screamed.

I dropped the champagne bottle and rushed to Michael. I put my ear to his blood-streaked back, listened for a heartbeat. Nothing. Not a sound. Only then did I realize that whoever had done this could not be far away. I stood upright and

looked around, my heart pounding. That was when I heard
footsteps descending the stairway. I rushed back out into the
hallway to the top of the stairs. I saw the slim back of a gray,
pin-striped suit topped by a full head of short brown hair
darting out my apartment door.

I ran downstairs to the house phone, called the doorman.
After several agonizing rings, Agron finally answered, "Yes, Mrs.
Quess?"

"There's a man coming down! Probably in the elevator now.
Gray suit, brown hair. Youngish, I think. You have to stop him!"

"What is your meaning?"

"STOP HIM, AGRON! He's just . . . uh . . . He just committed a *crime* up here."

I dodged using the word "murder." It was the first of several panic-driven mistakes.

"I should call the police?" Agron asked.

"There's no time. Just stop him! Then we'll get the police."

"But how do I know who this is?"

"GRAY suit, BROWN hair."

"I see two persons like that right now, Mrs. Quess. Make it
three. I see a gray suit coming in the front door right now."

"This one's coming *out* of the elevator."

"Two gray suits coming out of the elevator, Mrs. Quess. One
with pooch. Mr. Steenman from 712."

"The *other* one, then!"

"One with lady? Lady with poodle?"

"I don't know, Agron." *Would a murderer be traveling with a
lady and a poodle?* "Yes, stop him . . . Uh, ask him who he is."

"Okay. Hold tightly, Mrs. Quess."

I heard Agron's footsteps on the marble foyer floor, some voices, a laugh, then the footsteps again.

"Mrs. Quess?" Agron said.

"Yes."

"His name is Paley. Nicolas Paley. Was visiting his sister in 1010. He said this was first time a doorman ever ask him for his name on the way *out*."

What had I expected a murderer to say? "Was there . . . anything suspicious about him?"

"What is your meaning?"

"I don't know. Did he look nervous? Any blood on him?"

"Blood?"

"Yes, blood," I said.

"Do you need doctor, Mrs. Quess?"

"No, I'm fine."

"No. No blood on him, Mrs. Quess."

"Okay. Thank you, Agron." I started to hang up.

"Oh, Mrs. Quess?" Agron said. "He wasn't truly *with* lady with poodle. Just friendly talking, I guess. They walk away in different directions."

I should have called the police right then and there. Perhaps then things would have gone differently. Perhaps not. As Plutarch said, "History happens in spite of the choices we make." Or was it John Lennon who said that?

Instead, I crouched down on the carpet and bawled my eyes out. For Michael. For his wife and children. And of course, for me. The truth is, more than once I had imagined a man dying in my bed, although in a totally different way. Every time Abe Levanthal visits me, I have a fleeting vision of him conking out on top of me, taking his last gasp before his final orgastic yelp. For a man in his late sixties who has already suffered two heart attacks, Abe is an unusually athletic lover. He slaps on his nitro patch and goes at it like a tiger. Once I cautioned him to take it easy on his heart and he laughed and said, "What better way to go?" I asked him what I should do if he died in my arms and Abe said, "Call my son, Aaron. He'll take care of everything." Aaron is Abe's partner at Levanthal and Levanthal, attorneys-at-law.

I dialed Abe's cell phone number.

"Yes?"

"Abe, it's me, Lydia."

"It's ten-thirty. We're entertaining."

"It's an emergency, Abe."

"Wait," he said. He apparently walked into another room before speaking again. "You aren't supposed to have emergencies, Lydia. Everybody else in my life has emergencies. Ten, twenty a day. You are my oasis from emergencies."

"Somebody was murdered in my bedroom," I said.

"When?"

"I don't know. Twenty minutes ago."

"Not Paddy?"

"No, thank God. A . . . a client," I said. "Paddy's still out working."

"How? How was he murdered?"

"Stabbed in the back with an ice pick. While I was downstairs."

"Who did it?"

"I don't know. He ran away. A man, well dressed. He ran downstairs and out the door. I think he took the elevator down, but I'm not sure."

"Have you called the police?"

"No. Not yet."

"Good," Abe said.

"Good? Why good?"

"For the reason you haven't called them yet. Because you want to keep your personal damage to a minimum."

Abe was right about that, but I can't say it made me feel very good about myself. A man was just cut down in the prime of life and I was worried about keeping my personal damage to a minimum?

"I'll be right over," Abe said. "Don't do anything. Don't touch anything."

"I'm sorry about this, Abe."

"It's okay," he said. "What are friends for?"

Abe lives about thirty blocks north of me on Park Avenue, fifteen minutes away when traffic is light. I looked down at my watch, but of course, I wasn't wearing it. I wasn't wearing anything. Even though it was only Abe I was expecting, under the circumstances it did not seem appropriate to be walking around my apartment nude.

I made my way back up the stairs, each step an excruciating effort. About halfway up, I stopped. I kneeled on one step, lay my head sideways on another step. I wished I could have fallen asleep right there. Sleep is the most efficient mental escape

available to mankind, and I have always been a talented sleeper.
But the doorbell rang.

It couldn't be Abe yet. And Paddy rarely returned before
midnight from his Grand Central ministrations. My heart started
pounding in double time again.

"Who's there?"

"Me, Agron, Mrs. Quess. Just checking you up."

Dear, sweet Agron is a golden-hearted man. I have been
blessed with many in my life. Paddy says it is because I have
created a lifestyle that brings out the best in men.

"I'm fine, Agron. Thank you for asking."

"Did you call police?" Agron asked through the door.

"I, uh . . ." I hesitated. "It may not be necessary."

May not be necessary? Of course it was necessary! The only
question was *when* to call them. But now that Abe was on his
way, I was obligated to wait until he arrived to make the call.

"I forget to tell you one thing," Agron said.

"What's that?"

"The man with squeaky voice visiting his sister. He had a
rogue on."

"A rogue?"

"Wearing somebody else's hair."

"A rug," I said. Agron was taking a course in colloquial English at the Learning Annex.

"I hear buzzer. Doody calls," Agron said. "You call me if
you need me, okay, Mrs. Quess?"

"Okay, Agron. Thanks again."

The only way I could put on some clothes was by walking

through my bedroom to my closet. I stood outside my bedroom door planning my route. The object was to get in and out without laying eyes on the corpse on my bed. But of course, one step in and I was staring obsessively at Michael's body.

"I'm sorry, Michael," I whispered. "I am so very sorry. Please forgive me."

I was weeping. I grabbed the first items I saw in my closet—a tailored, button-down, blue oxford shirt, black slacks, Swedish clogs. My wardrobe did not change a whit when I switched professions. I am a conservative dresser by nature, although perhaps it is a holdover from my years in St. Elizabeth's plaid kilt, white blouse, and blue blazer uniform.

Out of habit, I checked my reflection in the closet's full-length mirror as I tucked my blouse into my slacks. I have no illusions about my body. I am thirty-three, slim, and fairly fit, and my breasts are smartly upstanding. But I am helped in this regard by the fact that they are quite small, B-minus cups. And I suffer from the same affliction that most American women do—my thighs are thick. You might think that this, combined with my too-long nose and off-kilter eyes (Raphael calls them my "Modigliani eyes") would put me at a disadvantage as a courtesan. But I refer you again to that winsome il Vecchio portrait at the Met. One's looks have very little to do with it.

The doorbell rang again just as I began to descend the stairs.

"Abe?"

"Yes."

"Be right there."

The first thing I noticed about Abe was that he was wearing a gray, pin-striped suit. I realized that was what he usually wore when he came by straight from his office—as did Frank and Michael too, for that matter. So that was hardly a telling bit of personal identification. Abe greeted me with a fatherly hug, not his usual manic clench that literally lifts me off my feet. I appreciated that. He headed straight for the stairs with me trailing right behind him. He stopped at the door to the bedroom and looked inside. He surveyed the scene silently for several minutes then, without turning, asked, "Who is he?"

"Michael Linscott," I said. "Michael Peabody Linscott the Third. He lives in Greenwich. Works at First Boston's New York office."

"Linscott? He did more than work there," Abe said. "He was their New York chief operating officer."

"You know him, Abe?"

"Not personally. Although I may have seen him somewhere. Yale Club, maybe. But I've heard of him. The banking world at that level is not that big." Abe turned to look at me. "Was he one of your regulars?"

There was a hint of jealousy in Abe's tone, a hint that he was doing his best to conceal. I appreciated both Abe's jealousy and his effort to conceal it. All my clients know I am not theirs exclusively, but that fact is never discussed. What I provide for them is equal parts fantasy and reality, as much dream as flesh. For their hours with me, I am indeed all theirs, and they like to sustain that illusion between their visits. Usually, it is not a problem for either of us, but at this moment there was no avoiding it.

"Yes, a regular," I replied.

"Let's have some coffee," Abe said.

Back downstairs, I made us both double espressos. We sat down at the kitchen table.

"Who knows about this besides you and me?" Abe asked.

"Nobody," I replied. "I mean, I told Agron there'd been a crime up here and to look for a brown-haired man in a pin-striped suit coming off the elevator. But I didn't say it was a murder and there's no reason for him to think it was."

"Did you speak to Agron face-to-face?" Abe reached across the table and lightly touched my cheek.

"No. Why?"

He scratched my ear, then held his finger up in front of my eyes. A rust-colored flake hung from his nail.

"Blood," Abe said. "Spots of it all over your left cheek, and on your ear."

Reflexively, I put my hand to my face, felt little dots of stickiness. My stomach wrenched. I swallowed hard to contain my nausea. "I . . . I put my ear on Michael's . . . his back," I stammered. "Listened for his heartbeat."

"I thought as much," Abe said. "Listen, whatever we do, I think you ought to wash that off right now."

I went to the kitchen sink and did as Abe instructed, scrubbing both cheek and ear with a sponge soaked in Palmolive Ultra. Abe then inspected my face through his bifocals, scratched a little more at my ear, and pronounced me clean. We sat down again.

"All right, here are the options," Abe said, his hands crossed in front of him on the table. "One, we call the police in a couple of minutes and you tell them exactly what happened. We'll leave out the ear-to-his-back business because it's irrelevant.

We explain the short delay in calling them for the genuine reason, that you wanted to consult with your lawyer first. This is Manhattan, so that won't sound particularly unusual."

I nodded.

"If we go that route, I will do what I can to keep as much of this out of the newspapers as possible. But there are no guarantees. Linscott is high profile. Not exactly a movie star, but a hell of a lot closer to one than, say, some Korean grocer in Queens who gets shot in a robbery. And the circumstances—Linscott's relationship to you—will make it particularly hard to keep a lid on it. This is what is known in the media as a sexy story." Abe offered me a rueful smile.

"What's option two?" I said.

"Two, we dispose of the body, his clothes, the sheets, the works. I know some people with experience in that sort of thing. So it all disappears and everybody goes on as if nothing happened. In a day or two, his wife will report him missing and then—"

"How the hell do you know people like that, Abe?"

"I represent them, on occasion."

"I HAD NOTHING TO DO WITH HIS MURDER!"

Abe shot up his palm to silence me. "I don't doubt that for a minute, Lydia," Abe said softly. "There's also not a doubt in my mind that, for a while at least, you will be a suspect. The *prime* suspect. And that everything about you will be investigated—your professional life, your income tax returns, undoubtedly your clients too."

"Are you worried about yourself, Abe?"

"A little, sure, but I'm more worried about you, Lydia," Abe said gently. "Much more. They'll do a real number on you. Even if they catch the perpetrator, they won't leave you alone. If there is one thing that infuriates police detectives, it is sex they can't afford."

I am pleased to report that our discussion ended right then and there.

"Fuck 'em," I said. Then I strode to the telephone and dialed 911.

2

Waiting miserably at the kitchen table for the police to arrive, I found myself thinking about Megan Marshak. I hadn't thought of her in years. Her lover, former Vice President Nelson Rockefeller, had a heart attack while lying heavily upon her naked young body. *Coitus interruptus termini.* Megan, like me, had called over a friend for a lengthy consultation before phoning the authorities. But that was not the part of the Megan-and-Nelson story that was playing in my mind.

I was in the sixth grade at St. Elizabeth's at the time of Rockefeller's climactic comedown, and I was already a news junkie, devouring all the New York newspapers—as well as *The National Enquirer* while my mother poked through the fruit bins at Stop-and-Save. Plus, even then I had a precocious talent for eavesdropping, say, in Vinny's Corner Newshop. Tales about the exact circumstances of Rockefeller's cardiac arrest were everywhere. The most popular—the one that ultimately flourished into legend—was that Rocky died lying face-up under a glass-topped table while Ms. Marshak hovered above it, making doo-doo.

I didn't believe it for a minute. Still don't. I imagine the people who invent these urban legends go on to fabulous careers at advertising agencies. But the point is, the longer Rockefeller's family and handlers tried to keep Megan Marshak out of the news, the more these legends prospered.

That was what I was thinking at the kitchen table.

I was also thinking I could probably manage to get on with my life if the precise nature of my relationship to Michael Linscott—that we had regularly enjoyed robust, adulterous sex and that I was paid for my participation—made the front page of, say, the *Post*. It would not be a surprise to any of my genuine friends. My father, thank God, had gone to his reward, my mother's Alzheimer's would protect us both, and as far as my brother and sisters were concerned, frankly, I didn't give a damn. But if a story began to circulate of me straddling a glass-topped table, doing number two for Michael's delectation below, I don't believe I would bear up very well. We all draw the line somewhere.

I wonder whatever happened to Megan Marshak.

The police arrived in a series of pairs. First, a couple of patrolmen on the local beat, one black, one Irish, what I later learned is known as a "salt-and-pepper" team. Both looked vaguely familiar from the neighborhood, and both possessed a no-nonsense, monosyllabic style reminiscent of *Hill Street Blues* reruns; perhaps that was where they'd learned it. Their designated tasks were to make sure the victim really was dead, and then to cordon off the bedroom as a crime scene. The latter was accomplished by stringing up wide, yellow tape emblazoned with the words CRIME SCENE—DO NOT CROSS every few feet in the upstairs hallway. The brightness of the yellow—a shade favored in sunny, suburban kitchens—struck me as cartoonish. Did New York cops routinely carry around a roll of this stuff? When they came home at the end of their shifts, did their kids sneak a roll out of their fathers' pants pockets and string the festive-colored tape around the walls of their playrooms? Abe and I silently watched the entire procedure from the bottom of the stairs.

Five minutes later a pair of plainclothes detectives arrived, also a salt-and-pepper combo. The black one was a good six-foot-five and probably weighed upwards of three hundred pounds. His name was Sergeant John Wilson, and after taking a quick survey of the crime scene, he left his partner upstairs and sat Abe and me down at the kitchen table, where he took out a spiral notebook and a pen.

What was my name? Did I live here? For how long? How old was I? What was the victim's name? Where did he live? How old was *he*? When did I observe that the victim had been assaulted? How long had the victim been out of my sight before I discovered that he had been assaulted?

"I don't know. Five minutes? Ten at the most."

"Did you hear a cry or any other sound that would indicate a violent act?"

"No. The CD player was on. Loudly. Downstairs, where I was," I replied.

Sergeant Wilson appeared to record every word I said, his mild, just-doing-my-job expression never varying.

"Are you married, Ms. Quess?"

"No."

"Have you ever been married?"

"No."

"There's a man's name next to yours on your buzzer," Wilson said.

"Paddy is my roommate," I said.

"Platonic?"

Were they reading Plato at the Police Academy these days? "Paddy and I are friends," I replied. "We have separate bedrooms. Paddy is a priest."

"Really?" Wilson's thick eyebrows rose ever so slightly.

"Yes, really."

"What kind of priest?" Sergeant Wilson asked.

"Roman Catholic." That was the short answer.

"Where is Father Riordin now?"

"Underneath Grand Central Station distributing food to the homeless. He should be back pretty soon."

"What was your relationship to the deceased, Ms. Quess?"

For the first time, Abe spoke up. "I do not believe Ms. Quess is required to answer that question," he said.

"And who are you?" Wilson asked.

"Abe Levanthal. Ms. Quess's attorney."

"How do you spell 'Levanthal'?"

Abe spelled it out.

"We were lovers," I blurted.

Abe glowered at me.

"You and Mr. Linscott, you mean," Sergeant Wilson said, flipping a page in his notebook as he spoke.

"Yes."

"And is Mr. Linscott married?" Wilson asked.

"Yes. And I do not believe Mrs. Linscott was aware of our relationship." Full disclosure, almost.

The radio phone attached to the detective's belt squawked. I couldn't understand a word that came out of it, but Wilson replied, "Send them right up," then said to us, "Forensics are on their way."

I nodded. Sergeant Wilson's calm thoroughness was reassuring. To me, at least. Abe's glower had developed into a glare that was clearly intended to make my responses more circumspect. I, on the other hand, believed that my responses had been remarkably circumspect so far.

"Who else knew about your relationship with Mr. Linscott?" Wilson asked.

"I don't know who Michael told, but Paddy knows," I said. "Father Riordin, that is."

Wilson began constructing some kind of diagram in his notepad with arrows extending from a small box at the center of the page.

"And . . . and a friend of mine," I went on. "Sylvia Kahn. A college friend. She, uh, she introduced us."

Wilson started to draw another little arrow, but Abe suddenly stood, bumping the table with his knees, which, in turn, caused the detective's pen to skitter off the page.

"We need to continue this interview at another time," Abe announced in an impressively lawyerly voice. "Perhaps tomorrow. My client is understandably upset right now."

"Where does Ms. Kahn live?" Wilson continued, not looking up.

"Riverside Drive," I said. "One twenty-five."

"That's it, Officer!" Abe barked. "End of interview!"

"Just one last question, please," Wilson said.

"Okay," I said.

"What line of work are you in, Ms. Quess?" Wilson asked.

"Private investments," Abe replied, clamping a firm hand on my shoulder.

"Is that a fact?" Sergeant Wilson said, flipping closed his notebook. "The market has really tanked lately, hasn't it, Ms. Quess?"

The door to my apartment swung open again and Paddy came bounding through, followed by two slim women about my age, both carrying large plastic valises. Paddy was wearing his usual working outfit—a clerical collar and dickey topped with a Yankees warm-up jacket, baggy jeans, and Doc Martens. His hair is a vintage Irish red that verges on orange, and his florid, somewhat beefy face gives the mistaken impression that he drinks Scotch all day long; in truth, he drinks it only after sundown. Paddy came straight at me, arms wide, and hugged me hard.

"This is terrible," he murmured.

"Thanks," I whispered back, holding on tight. Paddy's arms are the safest place I know, and I felt as if I might start crying again but managed to stave it off.

"You must be Father Riordin," Sergeant Wilson said.

Behind Wilson, the two valise-lugging women started up the stairs; they were clearly the forensics team. And behind me, Abe was on his cell phone, making reservations at the Sherry-Netherland. I had not thought that far ahead, but Paddy and I would need to spend the night somewhere else and Abe, ever the master planner, was already on it.

"That's me," Paddy said, disengaging himself from me and reaching out to shake Wilson's hand. "But I usually answer to 'Paddy.'"

"Okay, Paddy. I just need to ask you a few quick questions," Wilson said.

"He has the right to remain silent," Abe interjected.

Paddy smiled. "That's a right I've never felt like exercising before, so why start now? What do you want to know, Officer?"

Wilson wanted to know how well Paddy knew Mr. Linscott ("Only to say hello"), if he had known Mr. Linscott would be visiting me this evening ("Yes"), and if he knew that Mr. Linscott and I were engaged in "an adulterous relationship."

"Yes, I knew that," Paddy replied.

"And did you approve of that, Father?" Wilson asked.

Paddy smiled. "I am not in the judgment business, Sergeant," he replied. "Anyway, it's a crowded field."

At this point, Abe handed Wilson his business card, handed me a piece of paper with the hotel reservation number on it, and advised me again to keep my trap shut. Then he left.

I must say, I felt relieved when Abe exited. And a few minutes later, when one of the forensics ladies came downstairs to take my fingerprints, a swab of my saliva, and my "ear print" on a sheet of waxy paper, I was particularly glad that Abe was no longer there.

"I put my ear to Michael's . . . Mr. Linscott's back afterwards. To listen for a heartbeat," I explained preemptively.

"After what?" the woman asked.

"After I discovered he'd been stabbed."

"I see," the woman said. "But there's no sign of that on either of your ears. Or your cheeks, for that matter. The victim's back is covered with blood."

"I washed," I said. "I washed my face, my ears."

"Why did you do that, Ms. Quess?" Sergeant Wilson asked, his notebook out again.

"I don't know," I said. It was the first outright lie—other than lies of omission—that I had told Wilson, and I was not entirely sure why I said it. To protect Abe, who had advised me to wash up, assuring me it was irrelevant? "I guess because it upset me," I went on. "You know, his blood on my body."

"I see," Sergeant Wilson said. He was constructing a third little arrow in his diagram.

3

Paddy likes to call us soul mates. I say we are more like mirror images of one another, that I am the yin to his yang: He is a hopeless romantic and I am just hopeless. We met at a screening of *Romero* at Judson Memorial Church in the Village. This was during the period when I was struggling with what to do about my baby formula discovery, a time when I found myself attending lectures at the Ethical Culture Society, rereading Emerson, going to movies like *Romero,* and longing for a priest to talk to—a priest who wouldn't mind that I was a confirmed atheist, not to mention an adulteress. Paddy, of course, was that very priest.

Paddy remembered me from our Brooklyn neighborhood. I still can't place him from those days, although he swears he attended a parochial school one block from mine. He called to me by name after the screening, and we had an all-night talk in a Ukrainian eatery on Second Avenue. I learned that Paddy went straight from his parochial school to seminary, and straight from seminary to El Salvador, where he had been assigned a small village parish comprised almost entirely of impoverished coffee plantation workers and their families. There, he fell in with a group of "liberation" priests who had dedicated themselves to bettering the lives of their flock. In less than six months Paddy organized a strike, resulting in brutal military intervention. I listened as he told me of his several incarcerations in military prisons. It was an emissary from his Brooklyn diocese—with some leverage from the U.S. State Department—who finally brought him home.

By morning, I knew exactly what I had to do about my employer's barbarous business practices—in fact, I realized I had known all along, I had just lacked the guts to do it.

At that time Paddy was living with his parents for the first time since high school. His mother told him daily that he had broken her heart; his father told him daily that he was a bum. The next time Paddy and I met—for dinner at my house—I invited him to move in with me. "It is every St. Elizabeth's girl's dream to live with a priest," I said, grinning.

"I'm celibate, you know."

"I didn't know, but that's fine with me," I told him.

Paddy moved in later that week, the same week that I lobbed my first fistful of crapola into the corporate fan, and the same week that Paddy conceived of his mission as a free-floating minister to the homeless. It required an entire U-Haul truck to move Paddy in; his parents had meticulously packed cardboard boxes with everything Paddy had acquired over his thirty-one years. Paddy called it their exorcism; he never did unpack those boxes.

A few months later, Paddy confessed that like many other Salvadorian priests, he had taken a common-law wife, an Indian woman with whom, at the age of twenty-seven, he had had his first sexual experience. The love of this woman, he said, had brought him closer to God.

"I may never see her again, but I will always remain faithful to her," he told me. "So, you see, I'm not exactly celibate."

"Same difference," I said.

"No, there's all the difference in the world."

Abe had arranged for Paddy and me to have adjoining suites at the Sherry-Netherland—probably to the tune of a thousand dollars a night—but we ended up lying fully clothed, side by side, on a single bed in only one of those suites. It was past three in the morning by then, but neither of us could even think of sleeping.

"He must have been hiding somewhere upstairs," Paddy said. "In your closet, in my bedroom, in the bathroom? That's the only way he would have enough time to come into your bedroom and kill Michael while you were downstairs."

"Yes. That's what I think too."

"So when could he have come in and gotten up there?"

"It had to be *before* Michael came, right?" I said. "I mean, we were downstairs for a while and then went straight up to the bedroom. I can't think of any way someone could have come in during that time without us seeing him."

"When did you get home this afternoon?"

"I had lunch with Sira at the Grand Ticino. Left home at about noon and finished up around three. Then I went over to the Strand and browsed for maybe an hour. I picked up a copy of that new translation of *The Iliad* they're making such a big deal about. Had a Starbucks, stopped in at The New School to get their summer catalog—they've got that postmodern, post-structuralist hotshot from the University of Paris giving a course on Rimbaud in July. And then I came home. So that makes it what? Five-thirty? Six?"

"Let's call it five-thirty," Paddy said. "And what time did Michael arrive?"

"Seven. He's rarely late."

"What did you do between five-thirty and seven?" Paddy asked.

"Had a sandwich in the kitchen and read awhile. Then I took a bath and read some more. Everybody should read *The Iliad* in the bathtub for verisimilitude."

"So someone could have managed to get inside the apartment while you were bathing."

"I can't see how," I said. "The chain was up. I remember I unlatched it when Michael buzzed, then latched it again after I let him in. But the murderer must have unlatched it on his way out. He'd have to. Anyway, I remember noticing that it was unlatched when Agron rang the bell to ask if I was okay."

"Okay, so it's a fair guess that this man entered while you were out, between noon and five-thirty."

"But how? They installed those three-bolt megalocks last year. Supposed to be burglarproof unless the robbers bring a

blowtorch with them. And there was no sign of any forced entry that I saw."

"I don't know," Paddy said. "There are megalock experts, I
suppose. Professional second-story men probably take refresher
courses every now and then."

"At The New School."

"Right, from a post-structuralist hotshot," Paddy said.

We both chuckled. God knows, I needed a laugh, even a
little one. And nobody makes me laugh like Paddy.

"But it seems more likely that he got in with a key," Paddy
went on. "So who has a key besides you and me?"

"The super, I suppose. And Agron."

"Anybody else? Have you ever given one to any of your
friends?"

"No," I said. "I've had clients ask me for one, but I have a
rule against that. I'm a privacy freak, you know."

"I never noticed," Paddy said.

"You don't count, pal. You're my live-in confessor."

"Ever lend your key to anyone? That's all it takes to have a
copy made."

"No." I thought a moment. "Well, I did lend one to Michael
once because I knew I'd be late getting back for our date—you
know, when I was still taking Portuguese lessons uptown. But
that certainly doesn't help us. And once I lent a key to Sira.
About a month or so ago. She needed a place to tune up before an audition somewhere downtown."

Sira Patel is my former college roommate. A first-generation
American from an upper-class Bombay family, she'd arrived at
Barnard in a sari with a red dot in the middle of her forehead.

When she graduated, with a summa in musicology, her wardrobe was pure Bloomingdale's and the only red on her face was lipstick. Her parents tolerated that change only slightly more than her string of Jewish boyfriends. Sira now teaches at the Mannes School of Music and is a freelance harpist, which is surprisingly steady work. Currently, a harpist is *de rigueur* at posh weddings.

"And she gave it back to you afterward?" Paddy said.

"Right. She dropped it in the mailbox after she left."

"Well, that doesn't sound like a very promising lead."

"No. Not Sira."

"I, uh . . ." Paddy scratched at his jaw a moment before continuing. "I once lent my key to Manuel."

"When?"

"Couple weeks ago. I'd forgotten the vitamins, so I sent him back to get them."

"Oh, shit," I said.

Manuel has been Paddy's assistant in the Homeless Ministries for almost a year. He came to the job eminently qualified—homeless himself since he was fourteen. Paddy met him while doing his rounds of the Dumpsters around Chelsea Piers. Despite our offer to pay his rent in an apartment, Manuel chooses to remain in his Dumpster. I should note that a Dumpster near Chelsea Piers is considered a tony address among the homeless. Manuel, who likes to read the *New York* magazines he finds tossed into his Dumpster, says that for him it is a "lifestyle choice."

"I absolutely refuse to suspect Manuel of anything!" Paddy declared.

"On what grounds, Paddy?" I asked softly.

"Moral grounds. I trust him completely. It's a matter of faith."

"Paddy, *please!* Let's not even talk about this if you aren't going to be rational."

Paddy swung off the bed, lit up a Marlboro Ultra Light, and sat down in the Chippendale knockoff by the window. "Okay, I'll talk to Manuel," he said finally.

"Thanks. I'll talk to Sira too," I said. "Maybe we should try to get some sleep now?"

"Okay."

I kicked off my clogs. "Paddy? Who should I tell about this?"

"I was thinking about that too. Probably Frank and Raphael. And Sylvie too. It's better that they hear about it from you before some policeman comes knocking on their door."

I nodded. Tears started slipping down my cheeks again, the first time in hours. "I hate this," I said.

"I know. Me too." Paddy got back into the bed and I snuggled my head against his chest, where I quickly fell asleep.

4

"Frank? It's me, Lydia."

"Hi. Listen, I'm on the floor, so you'll have to make it quick."

"It's not a quick thing."

"It will have to be, darling."

"Okay. Somebody was murdered in my apartment last night and at some point I imagine the police will figure out what I do and with whom."

A very long pause. I could hear the staccato clicks and chatter of the Smith Barney trading room through the receiver, occasionally punctuated by an intelligible shout of "Pfizer!" or "News Corp!"

"We need to talk," Frank snapped when he spoke again. "Where are you?"

Now *I* paused. Paddy had risen early and brought back bagels and coffee from a Greek coffee shop four blocks away—

he simply couldn't bring himself to order up breakfast from room service, not when a pot of house coffee cost twelve dollars. I've never had the heart to tell him what my Starbucks habit costs. I took a bite of my bagel and chewed slowly. The truth is, I did not feel like having a face-to-face conversation with Frank Macy just now. He sounded even more tight-assed than usual.

"I am not at liberty to say," I said.

"*What?*"

No, not only did I not feel like having a face-to-face talk with Frank, I didn't feel like talking to him at all.

"Got to run," I said and hung up.

"How'd that go?" Paddy said. He had also bought the morning newspapers and was now scanning them for any mention of Michael Linscott's murder. So far, not a one.

"It is amazing how quickly a man cuts to the chase of self-interest when there's a crisis. Frank didn't seem overly concerned about my own situation. So I decided not to tell him where we are holed up."

"*Holed up?*" Paddy repeated, grinning. "I like the sound of that. 'Holed up' at the Sherry-Netherland."

"I just decided that I don't want Abe to be my lawyer either," I said. "I think he may have a conflict of interest."

"True," Paddy said. "Abe seems like a good man. We always have a nice chat when you're late. But he's got too much of his own at stake here."

"That means we'll have to give up our lovely rooms."

"Good, their cheesiness runneth over," Paddy said. "Listen,

Lydia, until we can go back into our place, maybe I should stay with my folks."

I could feel my lip tremble. "*You* aren't backing off from me too, are you?"

"Not on your life!" Paddy said, dropping his newspaper and coming over to plant a kiss on the top of my head. "I just don't want to cramp you. Like if you want to move in with Sari for a few days."

"I want us *both* to move in with Sari for a few days!" I said.

"That's two women, a harp, and a priest in a one-room apartment."

"That sounds like a joke, Paddy. Two women, a priest, and a harp walk into a—'"

The phone rang and I immediately picked up. "Hello?"

"Is this Lydia Quess?" A woman's voice, Boston vowels, brittle as glass.

"Who's calling, please?" But I could already guess.

"This is Angelica Linscott. Michael's widow."

Coming from Brooklyn, I have always been of two minds about the upper classes: On the one hand, I long to be one of them; on the other, I do not have the slightest idea what makes them tick. Make that *three* minds: I suspect they lack some essential human characteristics. Perhaps it's the result of centuries of inbreeding. But Michael had been dead for only twelve hours and Angelica Linscott was already referring to herself as his "widow" as if it were a patrician title she had recently acquired, albeit a title that carried with it some annoying social obligations.

"I am very sorry about your loss," I said as Paddy padded off to the bathroom.

"I believe we need to talk," Angelica replied evenly. "In person."

What was *this* about? Was she setting me up for something? A private meeting where she would gracefully withdraw a pearl-handled revolver from her beaded bag and shoot me once between the eyes? Or maybe the police would wire her so that she could extract some incriminating admission from me that would be recorded in a faux bread truck across the street. The latter seemed unlikely, not her style. Or maybe it was some arcane bit of social protocol we never learned in Brooklyn: the obligatory meeting between wife and mistress to work out the funeral arrangements? That would not completely surprise me.

"I can be in Manhattan by noon," she went on. "Let's make it lunch."

Lunch? The social protocol option was gaining credibility.

"Let me check my book," I said. Don't ask why. It just seemed like the appropriate response at the moment. But in fact, I did have a two o'clock appointment with Sergeant Wilson down at the Sixth Precinct, "to go over a few loose ends," as Wilson had put it.

"I'd have to leave by one-thirty," I said.

"That should be more than enough time," Mrs. Linscott said. "Should we make it the Oak Room? That's in your neighborhood."

"Fine," I said. Then, "How did you get this number, Mrs. Linscott?"

"Twelve o'clock then," she said and hung up.

As I put down the phone, I had one pressing thought on my mind: *What to wear?* I was well aware of the weightier issues at hand: A good man was dead; I had been sleeping with him; I was a prime suspect in his murder. Still, it was clearly in my best interest to give Mrs. Linscott the undeniable impression that I was a woman of both substance and style.

In other words, not a pushover.

Unfortunately, I had brought only one suitcase with me, and all it contained was a pair of beige cotton slacks, a chocolate brown cashmere sweater, my L.L. Bean lambskin slippers, and a change of underwear. Not exactly a showcase of elegance, any of it. Of course, there was the outfit I'd left my apartment in, slept in, and was still wearing—black wool slacks, oxford shirt, and clogs. Yet even freshly laundered, that ensemble would make a bigger statement at a business convention in Atlanta than it would at the Oak Room of the Plaza. But one item I *had* remembered to pack was my Saks Fifth Avenue credit card.

I made three quick calls, all of which were picked up by answering machines: on Sira's, I left a message asking if Paddy and I could crash for a few days; on Raphael's, I canceled tonight's date, promising to explain everything soon; and on Abe's—I'd phoned his answering service directly so I wouldn't have to speak with him in person—I asked him not to join me at the police station this afternoon, explanation to follow. That was when Paddy returned and I told him about my upcoming luncheon.

"It doesn't sound like something her lawyer would advise her to do," he said.

"Maybe she hasn't talked to her lawyer. It's not like she's a suspect herself."

"What makes you say that?"

"Well, first of all, we know he was killed by a man," I said.

"She could have hired him for the job."

"Paddy!" I was about to accuse Paddy of having a television-saturated imagination when I realized the scenario he was suggesting had as much merit as any at this point.

"In any event," I went on, "I can't see what *I* have to lose in meeting with her. And I'm not consulting my lawyer because, as of a few minutes ago, I don't have one."

"And let's face it, you're curious as hell," Paddy said. "Which, incidentally, makes two of us."

I scrubbed my face and did my eyes, then changed into my clean slacks and sweater, slipped back into my clogs, picked up my pocketbook, and started for the door. I was going shopping.

"I'll leave with you. I have a luncheon date myself," Paddy said. "I'll meet you in front of the police station at two, okay?"

"Who are you lunching with?"

"Some friends. At the soup kitchen behind the bus terminal."

"Yin and yang go to lunch," I said bravely, although I was feeling unexpectedly apprehensive about being separated from Paddy for even a few hours.

5

There is nothing like a stroll down Fifth Avenue—say, between Fifty-Ninth and Fiftieth Streets—to lull yourself into the illusion that all's well with the world, that God's earth is a bountiful place populated exclusively with good-looking people. It is a world made in capitalist heaven: just shops and shoppers.

A few years back, some clever young designer at Saks created a series of high-kitsch window dioramas inspired by *The Threepenny Opera*. They depicted scenes of the Beautiful People decked out in Gaultier and Boss while dirty-faced beggars in rags stared wide-eyed at them from the corners of the windows. The *Times* deemed the display the height of bad taste, but Paddy and I thought it was terrific. "Brecht would be thrilled," Paddy had said when we came uptown to see it for ourselves.

The clever young designer was fired.

I took the escalator up to Saks's designer boutique, where I made a beeline for a no-nonsense-looking saleswoman.

"I'm a six and I need something for lunch," I greeted her.

"Where?" she asked.

"The Oak Room."

"Step this way."

She led me straight to the Rena Lange collection. There, she gave me a well-practiced once-over, then made directly for a rack of skirt suits, where she selected one and held it up for my inspection. It was a navy blue boucle tweed with a knee-length skirt (solving the thigh problem) and a Peter Pan collar on the jacket. The collar was the clincher: It said boyish *yet* sexy, innocent *yet* self-assured. All in all, it was fittingly reminiscent of my St. Elizabeth's uniform. That is, except for the price tag that hung discretely from the left sleeve: $2,790.00.

I nodded approval and she led to me a dressing room. While I was still undressing, she returned with a pair of silk stockings and black leather pumps. Exactly fifteen minutes after I arrived at Saks, I emerged from the dressing room looking like a princess from a small middle-European principality. Or at least from Greenwich. And that was when a man in chinos and a bush jacket snapped my picture.

He had been crouching behind a mannequin that sported a Jean Paul Gaultier chain collar shirt—the *haute* bondage look—waiting for me. And he didn't take just one picture; he took at least a dozen, in rapid, machine-gun-fire pops.

"What the hell are you doing?" I snarled.

He immediately turned away and made for the escalator.

The saleslady took my credit card and rang up my purchases without any acknowledgment of my little scene. When you have sold three thousand dollars' worth of merchandise in fifteen minutes flat, you tend to ignore a few flashbulbs and a little snarling. I asked her to put the clothes I'd changed from into a bag, which I would pick up some other time.

Angelica Linscott was waiting for me in the Plaza lobby. I recognized her from a family photo Michael had shown me: about five-nine, very thin, and naturally blond. In fact, her blond hair, pale skin, broad forehead, straight features, and smallish blue eyes made her look like a close blood relative to her late husband. Maybe that had been part of Michael's problem: Bedding her felt too much like incest. But then again, perhaps the two only looked similar to me. The way all Brooklyn-bred, Irish Catholic girls probably look alike to her, even in Rena Lange skirt suits.

Mrs. Linscott extended her hand to me. "My God, you don't even have any tits to speak of."

It was not the greeting I had expected, but I must say it immediately put me at my ease.

"I am sure we have lots in common, Mrs. Linscott," I replied, smiling.

"Call me Angelica," she said.

"Of course."

The *maître d'* led us to a table for two under the fronds of a gigantic potted palm.

"Asparagus is still in season," Angelica said as we took our seats.

I gazed across the table at her. Her conversational style made me suspect everything she said was fraught with clever double meanings; the word "asparagus" had already called to mind a whole litany of graphic gags from my St. Elizabeth days about nuns crouched in asparagus patches. But if Angelica was showing off her wit, I certainly couldn't tell from her facial expression. Note the singular: She appeared to have only one; it fell somewhere between bemused and patronizing.

"How are your children bearing up?" I asked.

"We haven't told them yet," she replied, signaling for a waiter.

I knew both of their children were at boarding school, but *still*. Why was she here, rather than off to Choate to bring them the news? And who was this *"we"* who hadn't told them yet? The waiter arrived, Angelica ordered the asparagus salad, and I requested the fruit cup appetizer.

"Dieting?" Angelica said.

"I had a late breakfast," I replied.

"Okay, first the books," Angelica said. "I will send them to your apartment."

"What books?"

"The French books. Three of them. Baudelaire, Zola, and the journals of somebody or other I have never heard of. First editions, I gather. I imagine they are worth something."

Occasionally, when Michael returned from a business trip abroad, he brought me back a rare book or two. I kept a couple, but sold most of them on eBay to keep Homeless Ministries in clover.

"You are very kind," I said.

"Apparently it was a little hobby you got him interested in. Perhaps he was planning to give them to you sometime. In any event, he left them to you."

"In his will?"

"Yes."

No time to tell the children, just enough to read the will.

"Thank you so very much," I said. What lovely manners I have.

"I don't know who did this," she said. "But I certainly hope they find him soon."

I was struck by her use of the masculine pronoun; apparently, the Widow Linscott did not believe that I was a suspect. I appreciated that, but what reason did she have *not* to suspect me?

"Me too," I said.

"In the meantime," Angelica went on, "you and I share a dicey public relations problem."

Aha! The meeting will now come to order.

"His infidelity," I said.

"Goodness no," Mrs. Linscott said, laughing. "Men of Michael's standing are expected to do that here and there. A gentleman's hobby, like collecting French books."

"What is the problem then?" I said. I was about to ask if the fact that Michael had paid cash for his hobby was the sticky wicket, as it were, but I decided to hold back.

"Dr. Kahn is the problem," Mrs. Linscott said.

"Dr. Kahn?"

"Yes, the last thing in the world we want is Sylvia gabbing

with the police. Or, heaven help us, going on *Oprah* or something. You know how psychologists are. Incurable narcissists."

Angelica ever so slightly raised the corners of her thin-lipped
mouth. Clearly, I had underestimated her facial repertoire.

"Heaven forbid, *Oprah*," I said, trying valiantly to filter every
ounce of sarcasm out of my voice. I so wished Paddy could
have been at the next table, eavesdropping on every word.

"It could make a terrible mess," the widow said.

"But maybe Dr. Kahn has information that can help the investigation," I ventured.

"I cannot imagine what that would be," she replied—not
entirely convincingly.

Obviously, Mrs. Linscott knew her husband had been
Sylvie's patient and that I had been a critical part of his treatment. But beyond that, what? Did she know Michael had continued to see me long after he had been "cured"? Clearly, she
knew he had been in my bed last night, but did she know it
was no longer on doctor's orders? And if so, what difference
did that make to her anyway, it being a gentleman's hobby
and all?

"I still don't quite get what the problem is," I said.

"Don't you?"

I suddenly realized this was not a rhetorical question. Angelica was fishing! She was trying to determine how much I
knew about something that involved Sylvia Kahn. And she was
hoping I *didn't* know a thing about it. But what could that be?
Something she was afraid that Michael had confided in me?
That would probably be something about Angelica herself . . .
I decided to take a flying guess.

"You mean, about *your* professional connection to Dr. Kahn," I said in a neutral voice.

Bingo! Mrs. Michael Peabody Linscott III blanched.

"You, of all people, should be able to see this from a feminist perspective," Mrs. Peabody said after a moment.

Oh, dear, the *feminist perspective.* I am all for gender equality, feminine empowerment, the whole ball of wax, but I had a sneaking suspicion that Mrs. Linscott's brand of feminism had a lot more to do with self-interest than with, say, leveling the playing field for underpaid working mothers.

"Try me," I said.

"As you know, Michael had his problem and I had mine," she said.

I nodded, waiting. But Angelica was also waiting—again waiting to see just how much I knew already. Time for another flying guess. But this time, as I studied Angelica's remote blue eyes, I felt more sure of myself.

"If men have orgasms, we should be able to have them too," I said. "It's only fair."

"I knew you would understand." She looked tremendously relieved.

The ducks were positively jostling with each other to get into line. So Angelica had seen Sylvia also, for an elusive Big O. And what had Sylvia prescribed—say, after estrogen patches and Kegel exercises failed to do the trick? Were there also male sex surrogates? Sylvia had never mentioned them to me. *But why shouldn't there be?*

This *was* a feminist issue, after all!

I'd bet the farm that not only had Mrs. Linscott received

treatment from a sex surrogate, but she had become as enthralled by him as Michael had with me. She, too, had continued to visit him long after she had been cured of her sexual shortcoming. As I say, Masters and Johnson must have been sniffing glue not to have forseen that little wrinkle in their procedure. Had Michael and Angelica agreed on what was called, in more enlightened times, an "arrangement"—you see your surrogate, I see mine?

I was beginning to see why this might be a social problem for Mrs. Linscott.

Feminism has its limits—especially as you head north on the Connecticut Turnpike. A gentleman's infidelity is one thing, even a gentleman who pays for it; even, presumably, a gentleman whose infidelity was sponsored by a sex therapist. But a woman—a *Greenwich* woman—who regularly has her brains fucked out by a proficient sex surrogate so she can finally have the orgasm of her dreams? That undoubtedly crossed the line— the line that separates tennis club ladies of good standing from women of questionable character. Angelica was desperate to stay on the right side of the line. For the moment, keeping everything under wraps trumped mourning her late husband or dealing with her children.

"I was hoping you might talk to Sylvia," Mrs. Linscott continued. "I understand you were at Bar*nard* together."

The way in which she enunciated "Barnard" made me think Angelica had not attended an A-list college herself.

"Yes. We go way back," I said. I deliberately did not commit myself to a *tête-à-tête* with Sylvia. I wanted to verify my guesses, so I was saving that in case I needed leverage. I leaned across the table and said softly, "Your friend. The one Sylvia arranged for you. Can you think of any reason he would want Michael dead?"

Mrs. Linscott sat up very straight. Her salad had arrived and she grasped the end of an asparagus spear between her forefinger and thumb, dangled it in front of her aristocratic face, and chomped off its head. Now I am pretty sure that Angelica was unfamiliar with the old St. Elizabeth's asparagus gags, but surely, given the subject at hand, she could see the symbolism in the mouth work she was giving that asparagus.

"No reason at all," she said after she'd finished chewing. She patted her lips with a napkin. "He doesn't have a violent bone in his body."

"I'll try to see Sylvia today," I said.

"Good."

I looked at my watch. Time to make my way to the Sixth Precinct.

"How did you know to find me at the Sherry-Netherland?"

"Sergeant Wilson let it slip."

Wilson didn't strike me as a man who would let anything slip, unless he was doing some fishing himself.

"Oh, there was one other thing I was wondering about, Angelica," I said as I gathered up my pocketbook. "You said this was a public relations problem that we *shared*. What exactly is *my* public relations problem?"

"Are you joking with me, dear?" she asked.

"There's no way the police won't find out what kind of work I did on Dr. Kahn's behalf. My talking with her won't change that."

"Are you quite sure?" she said, pantomiming to the waiter for the check. He arrived in an instant.

"I'm afraid I'm late for an appointment," I said, reaching into my purse for my wallet.

"Please!" Angelica said, extending her hand to stop me. "For one little fruit cup? Don't embarrass me."

She signed the check—obviously a regular customer—and trilled her fingers at me as I rose to leave.

"Ta-*tah*!" I said. I had learned that at Barnard.

6

In the cab going downtown, I did a quick review.

I only asked Mrs. Linscott if she thought her "friend" might be a murder suspect as camouflage for verifying that he *existed*. But I may have been on to something. It was fair to surmise Mrs. Linscott's prescription lover not only *knew* that she was married, but also that she was married to a very *rich* man. From my experience, that is the kind of personal information that does not stay secret long once you take off your underwear. And you don't have to watch a lot of television to be able to know that a rich husband is a plausible motive for murder.

Whoa, girl! Consider your assumptions here. A big fat one was that any man who screws for dollars was quite capable of murdering for dollars. *Where did that come from?* Was I detecting a little latent sexism of my own? That any *male* sex surrogate had some serious morality issues? Unlike me, of course, who was constitutionally incapable of hurting a fly because, well, I was a member of the gentler sex. I had not even entertained the possibility that the man had fallen in love with Angelica, pure and simple. But what if he had? That was *also* a time-honored motive for husband-killing! So, any way you looked at it, Angelica's loverboy deserved a spot on the suspects list. And what about Mrs. Michael Peabody Linscott III herself? Did she belong on the list too, as Paddy had suggested?

As the cab took the turn onto Tenth Street, I noticed a bank clock that said it was exactly five minutes before two. Five minutes to the hour is the optimum moment for calling shrinks, a little window between patients. I dialed Sylvia on my cell phone.

"Dr. Kahn."

"Sylvie? It's me, Lydia."

"Jesus Christ!"

Obviously, she knew about the murder. "Yeah, where is He when you need Him, right?"

"Well, you seem perky for a, uh—"

"I believe 'murder suspect' is the term you are looking for, Doctor."

"You sound manic, Lydia," my friend, the therapist, said soberly.

"Yes, well, consider the alternative."

"Lydia, this is serious stuff. We all have to be very, very careful," Sylvia said.

"That's what everybody seems to be saying today," I replied. "Except for Michael Linscott, of course."

"Lydia, do you have any Xanax?"

Actually, that was a reasonable question—not whether I had any Xanax, but why was I carrying on so flippantly with her. Sure, Sylvie and I have been bantering with each other since we were freshmen; she had been my very first sister-wiseguy. But something else was going on. I wasn't quite ready to talk seriously with her about the Linscotts.

"Actually, no," I said to Sylvia.

"I'll have Prassad call in a prescription right away."

"Thanks," I said.

"No problem," Sylvia said, and she abruptly hung up.

Obviously, Sylvia didn't want to have a serious conversation with me either.

Paddy was waiting for me in front of the police station as promised.

"How'd lunch go?" he asked.

"Fascinating," I said. "Long story."

"I meant the food," Paddy said, winking as he took me by the arm.

"I wasn't hungry. How about yours?"

"The usual. Pea soup and franks. Sometimes I think the people who plan soup kitchen menus are intent on making the homeless smell even worse."

I was laughing as we entered the station house. That was unfortunate, because Sergeant Wilson was waiting for me just inside the door, and what he saw was his personal, number-one murder suspect laughing gaily as she strode in wearing a brand-new and expensive-looking outfit. Sylvia was right: It was time to become a little more cautious.

Wilson nodded formally to both of us, then led the way to a small, windowless office in the rear of the building. There, he introduced us to an attractive Asian woman in a smart, dark blue uniform that looked remarkably like my new suit— tailored knee-length skirt, short-collared sky blue shirt, and tapered jacket. Subtract the badges and stripes and you'd think Rena Lange had been moonlighting. The woman's name was Captain Amy Liu. She shook Paddy's and my hands perfunctorily before telling us to sit down.

"Do you wish to wait for Mr. Levanthal before we begin?" she asked.

"No. I am no longer retaining him," I said.

Liu and Wilson exchanged quick, professional-looking glances—the kind that said, "Note that, but don't react to it."

"Will somebody else be representing you then?" Liu said.

"I don't know," I said. "Why? Do I need a lawyer?"

"It is your right to have one," she said.

"Does that mean I am a suspect, Captain Liu?" Might as well be absolutely clear about things from the get-go.

"No one has been eliminated."

"Meaning?"

"Meaning we are still investigating, Ms. Quess," Liu said.

"And how is the investigation progressing, Captain?" Paddy asked. I wouldn't absolutely swear to it, but I thought I detected a hint of a Dublin brogue in his voice. Which was perfectly ridiculous, considering he is third-generation Brooklyn.

Consciously or not, Paddy must have thought it went with his role—the kindly Irish padre from a forties Boystown movie softening up the cops.

"So far, so good," Liu said.

"For what it's worth, I figure the killer must have been hiding in my apartment for a long time before he did it," I said. "Let himself in while I was out, which was between noon and five-thirty or six."

"Could be," Liu said.

"And Agron—the doorman—saw a man who fit his description coming off the elevator just minutes after the murder."

"Yes, he told us that," Liu said.

"So did your forensics people pick up anything?" I said. "Fingerprints? Shoe prints?"

"They picked up all kinds of things," Captain Liu said. "Nothing on the murder weapon itself, but bits and pieces of DNA all over the place."

"That sounds promising," I said.

Captain Liu pursed her lips and took a slow, deep breath, the kind that recently reformed smokers take reflexively.

"Judging by the lab findings, there seemed to be a lot of traffic in your bedroom, Ms. Quess," she said. "Do you entertain often?"

"Fairly often."

"In your bedroom, I mean."

"I know where you meant."

"And do you . . . know all of these visitors personally?" Captain Liu asked with—forgive me—an inscrutable smile.

I considered giving the captain a *what-kind-of-woman-do-you-take-me-for* glare, but I didn't know how much she already knew. "Yes, I do," I said.

"I am going to have ask you for their identities," Liu said.

I admired her choice of words—not their names and their addresses, but their *identities*. Very existential. Maybe they also read Sartre at the Police Academy.

"I can do that," I said. "That is, if you can assure me you will treat this information confidentially. I don't want their families to know about their relationship to me. Or their colleagues. And certainly not the newspapers."

"And I can guarantee that," Liu said.

"But we can't give you assurances about anybody else talking," Sergeant Wilson said.

"I understand," I said. *Like your little "slip" to the Widow Linscott.* For the first time since I'd left Saks, I thought about the photographer who had ambushed me. Who knew who was saying what to whom already?

Wilson removed a yellow legal pad from a desk drawer and handed it to me along with a pen. I wrote down Frank, Abe, and Raphael's full names, their addresses, and their private phone numbers. They were the only other men who had been in my bedroom for several months now. I returned the pad to Wilson.

"But what about footprints or shoe impressions or whatever you call them?" I said. "*Fresh* footprints."

"Yes, we got some of those, for what they are worth," Liu said. "So far, all they give us is a fairly common shoe brand, style, and size. Nothing more. No tissue."

"But you could tell they were fresh, right?"

"We could tell they were made within the previous twelve hours," Wilson said. In other words, the shoe impressions did nothing to corroborate my account of the fleeing brown-haired man.

"And that man the doorman saw coming off the elevator— any leads there?" I said.

"He saw two men," Wilson said. "Mr. Steenman, from Apartment 712. I've spoken with him. And a Mr. Paley, who told the doorman he was visiting his sister in 1010," Wilson said.

"Yes, that one."

Once again, Liu and Wilson exchanged shorthand glances.

"We have not been able to locate him. But Mrs. Thorpe in 1010 does not have any living brothers," Liu said.

"Terrific!" I said. "I mean, that must be the man. The killer. Why else would he lie?"

"I could give you about fifty reasons off the top of my head, Ms. Quess," Wilson said. "Like he didn't want anybody to know who he *really* spent his evening with. Or why."

Captain Liu eyed Paddy for a moment, then said to me, "Are you a prostitute, Ms. Quess?"

Now it begins. "It depends on your definition," I said.

"I should say that if you are, Ms. Quess, there is absolutely no reason why I would need to report this to vice or to anyone else. It would simply be helpful in our investigation."

Okay, here is what I was thinking: How can I tell the truth while keeping my "personal damage" to a minimum? Not to mention Frank, Raphael, Abe, and even Michael's personal damage. In other words, how could I be *very, very careful*?

So I explained to Captain Liu my arrangement with Dr. Sylvia Kahn, duly licensed sex therapist. I made it sound as if Frank was lumped in with the others, and I omitted the fact that all of these patients were currently doing postgraduate sessions with me. As I spoke, I could see Sergeant Wilson was struggling manfully to keep from rolling his eyes. I could also see that Amy Liu was hanging on every word. Paddy, God love him, just sat there nodding and occasionally patting my hand.

"It is a form of therapy then," Liu said after I had finished. "Like physical therapy."

"A perfect analogy," I said, although I was beginning to feel more hypocritical than was comfortable. I was publicly forsaking my courtesan pride.

"And Dr. Kahn," Liu continued matter-of-factly. "I assume she receives some kind of fee for her referrals. Like an orthopedist does from a physical therapist that he recommends."

"Yes."

"How much would that be, Ms. Quess? Ten percent? Twenty? Fifty?"

"Twenty-five," I said.

"Well, there's a difference right there," Captain Liu said, looking me steadily in the eye.

"From what?"

"A madam takes a sixty percent cut," Liu said. "Often more."

In spite of myself, I liked Amy Liu's style. I liked the way she paced her questions, inching in incrementally.

"Medicine has a long history of making sin respectable," I said. "Take Prozac, for example. Shouldn't a drug that makes a person feel that good be illegal?"

Wilson offered Liu another conspiratorial glance—this one saying, "We've got ourselves a screwball, Captain"—but Amy wasn't buying. I believe she was enjoying this little colloquy as much as I was. "Are you suggesting that medicine can be immoral?" she said.

"Just the opposite," I replied. "I think medicine, in its own clunky way, is often wiser than conventional morality."

"And wiser than conventional *laws*?" Amy Liu asked.

"On occasion."

From the corner of my eye, I could see Paddy was beginning to get nervous. He knew from experience that once I got cooking in a rousing philosophical argument, my personal judgment flew out the window. He was right. It made me doubly glad that Abe was not there.

"Are you saying that all prostitution should be legal?" Liu said.

"Absolutely," I said. "Although it probably should be supervised. The way they do in France and Holland. To keep sexually transmitted diseases under control."

Captain Liu smiled very scrutably. "Correct me if I am wrong, Ms. Quess, but at least one thing you are saying is that there is really no difference between the service you provide for Dr. Kahn's patients and what a Forty-Second Street hooker does for a living. Is that right?"

Damn, Amy Liu was good! She was far sharper than I'd thought a cop could be. I suppose I was far smarter than she thought a prostitute could be.

"Right," I said. "No difference at all. Except the price tag. And the level of conversation my clients have come to expect."

Saying that, I immediately felt relieved. I'd gotten my courtesan pride back. I realized this was a discussion I'd been wanting to have with somebody—some *woman*—for a long time. Like with my friend, Sira. Or with Sylvia. But for some reason, I had always shied away from it.

Captain Liu offered me a quick, ceremonial-looking bow and I returned it. *Crouching Tiger, Hidden Dragon* at the Sixth Precinct.

Sergeant Wilson broke the spell. "Do you own an ice pick, Ms. Quess?"

"No."

"How about you, Father?"

"No, I don't," Paddy said. No brogue this time. "I mean, not at our apartment. We—my parents—do have one at home in Brooklyn, though."

This instantly struck me as more information than was necessary.

"Describe it," Wilson said.

Paddy shrugged. "I'm not sure. Wooden handle, I think. Yes, an unvarnished wooden handle. And, you know, the metal pick—the awl. It's old. They've had it since I was a kid."

"Is there anything written on the handle?" Wilson said. "A brand name or something?"

"Yes, I think the name of a bar or a restaurant. Must have been a handout or door prize from back when restaurants did that sort of thing."

"Kedding's?" Wilson said. "Kedding's Bar and Grill?"

Paddy's already ruddy face reddened some more.

"Maybe. I really can't remember," Paddy said softly.

What was this *about?*

"Did you kill Michael Linscott, Father?" Wilson asked.

"No," Paddy said, shaking his head. "Of course not."

"Can anyone verify your whereabouts at the time of the crime?"

"My assistant, Manuel, and about a hundred mole people," Paddy said. "Mole people" was what the homeless living below the streets called themselves.

"And you, Ms. Quess? Did you kill him?"

"Don't be ridiculous!" I shouted. Not the most prudent manner in which to answer, but I was not feeling prudent. I was feeling panicked.

"Who do you think did kill him?" Captain Liu asked.

"I don't know," I said. "Isn't the wife the usual suspect?"

"The wife *or* the lover," Liu said. "In this case, the wife can account for her whereabouts."

"So can the lover," I said.

"*Exactly,*" Sergeant Wilson said.

Liu abruptly stood, signaling the end of our interview. "We'll need at least one more day in your apartment. In the meantime, remain in the city and always let us know where we can reach you." She started to hand me her card, then stopped to scribble something on it. "I'll give you my cell number too," she said, offering me another one of those smart little ceremonial bows.

7

Abe Levanthal was waiting for us outside the station house, his fireplug frame leaning against the trunk of his limo.

"I think you have a death wish," was his greeting.

"No matter, I've had a good life," I replied. I was not at all pleased to see him, but it didn't surprise me. Abe is not a man who takes rejection—personal *or* professional—lightly.

"You don't have any idea what's in play here, Lydia," he said, walking toward Paddy and me. "I think you are under the mistaken impression that if you are innocent, you have nothing to worry about."

Basically, I *was* under that impression. Although that ice-pick "Q and A" a few minutes ago had given this belief a good shake.

"The police operate under a very simple principle: Get a conviction and close the case," Abe continued. "Upon this are promotions won and pay grades increased. It has nothing at all to do with getting the right man."

If I had not just made the acquaintance of Captain Liu of the Homicide Division, I might have given Abe's pronouncement more consideration. But there was not a doubt in my mind that Amy Liu had an omnivorous appetite for the truth. And judging by her rank, it hadn't hurt her career one bit.

"You'd have a conflict of interest if you represented me," I said to Abe.

"I can compartmentalize these things," he replied, with one of his least-attractive smiles.

"Really?" I said.

"Believe me, Lydia, I only have your best interest at heart," Abe said, tenderly reaching out to touch the side of my face.

Since we were standing directly in front of the windows of the Sixth Precinct, his gesture seemed foolhardy to say the least. A public display of affection with your client? Abe must have at least *suspected* that the police now knew about his extralegal relationship to me. You would think he was actually trying to *ensure* that he could not possibly represent me. I got a jolt of the same feeling I'd experienced when Sylvia sounded eager to get off the phone with me. It was still early in the day and I'd already had a double dose of the infamous loyalty of rats on a sinking ship.

I took a step backward; Abe's hand dropped from my face.

"I'll contact you if I think I need to, Abe," I said.

"I hope you mean that," he said. He leaned his mouth to my ear. "Are we still on for Thursday night?" he whispered.

I burst out laughing. I wish I could say it was a cruel-sounding laugh—heaven knows, that was what Abe deserved. But it was just a plain-old laugh at the absurdity of the male condition. My favorite Lenny Bruce routine is the one about a guy bleeding to death in the back of an ambulance; the EMT nurse leans over him to mop his brow and the dying man says, "Great tits, lady."

"I need to take some time off, Abe," I replied. "Don't call me, I'll call you."

Abe looked crestfallen. The murder had finally struck home—it was interfering with his sex life.

Paddy and I started off in the direction of Sixth Avenue, neither of us speaking for several minutes. Finally, I said, "What was that about your parents' ice pick? You seemed to go out of your way to bring it up."

Paddy nodded soberly. "I took a quick peek inside your bedroom before we left last night. I saw the ice pick. Still in his back. The forensics team had set up high-intensity lamps and were photographing it from all different angles. That light-colored wooden handle—it rang a bell."

"That doesn't make any sense, Paddy. There have got to be a million ice picks that look like that in this city. Why even mention—?"

"I know, I know," Paddy said. "Doesn't make any sense at all."

"Unless there's something you aren't telling me."

"No. Nothing," Paddy said.

Did Paddy hesitate a nanosecond before his denial?

"So tell me about Mrs. Linscott," Paddy said.

I told him the entire story.

"Maybe you should talk to Sylvia today," he said.

"I'm sure Sylvie will cooperate with Captain Liu no matter what I say. In fact, I sincerely hope she does." I took a deep breath. "I just want this damned thing solved, Paddy. No matter what it takes."

"Me too," Paddy said. "But who knows? Maybe Sylvia will tell you something she wouldn't say to the police."

"I doubt it," I said. "But what if she does? What do I do with it?"

"I don't know." Paddy shrugged. "But maybe Abe's right. It's a mistake to think that just because you're innocent, you have nothing to worry about."

I stopped short and looked hard into Paddy's eyes.

"I don't like the sound of that," I said.

"Neither do I," Paddy said. He kissed me on the cheek and headed downtown for an appointment with his beef jerky connection.

Rather than phone Sylvia again, I decided to crash her Eighty-Fifth Street office. I asked the cabbie to take the West Side Highway uptown; I might just make the five-minutes-to-three window.

The first time I ever laid eyes on Sylvia Kahn, I giggled. That was fifteen years ago in freshman composition class. The teacher, a Columbia graduate student who reminded us daily that she would much rather be working on her thesis, was lecturing about her compositional pet peeves. At the top of that list were double negatives. She said (for the second time) that using a double negative was a sign of negative thinking.

"Yeah, yeah," Sylvie crowed back in a bored voice.

"And what is that supposed to mean, Ms. Kahn?" the teacher asked.

"It's a double affirmative," Sylvie replied brightly.

I waited for Sylvia after class. I needed this girl to be my friend.

Indeed, Sylvia and I became great friends, although in a different way from Sira and me. While Sira and I indulged that adolescent urge to bare every fiber of our barely formed personalities to each other, Sylvia and I talked exclusively about the books we were reading and the plays and poetry readings we attended together. Hardly a word was spoken about our families or our other friends, female or male.

At seventeen, Sylvie had already developed a pitch-perfect Dorothy Parker–esque wit. Caustic cracks tripped off her tongue in virtually every class we took. My favorite was when that same composition teacher wondered out loud why her male Columbia students needed to use far fewer adjectives than her Barnard students did; replied Sylvie in a heartbeat, "Because they are unmodified pricks." In one rare moment of personal candor, Sylvie told me that she considered herself a kindred spirit to Dorothy Parker because they were both half-Jewish. "Our whole *lives* are *double entendres*," she'd said.

We lost touch with one another after college. She had a Fulbright in France; I had Harvard Business School. We didn't hook up again until five years ago when we ran into each other at an opening in a Soho gallery. When I first glimpsed

Sylvie, I barely recognized her: She'd lost a good thirty pounds and her features looked much softer. But most disguising was her outfit: Sylvia Kahn, the girl who had bragged that she wore the same pair of jeans every day for her entire senior year, was dressed to kill in a de la Renta party dress. She ran the length of the gallery to embrace me.

"God, I've missed you," she said.

"It's great to see you too," I said. "You look terrific, by the way."

"Amazing, no?" Sylvie laughed. "I've been born again. Glory be modern surgery!"

"On you it looks good, Sylvie."

A tall, cocoa-colored man with a confident, toothy smile appeared at her side. He looked Indian or Pakistani and his longish black hair and rakish black eyes attracted appreciative glances from the assembled art lovers.

"Lydia, I'd like you to meet my husband, Prassad Panaik," Sylvie said. "*Doctor* Prassad Panaik, actually."

I did my level best to keep my grin under control. Sylvia Kahn seemed so proud of her marital accomplishment; she wore her handsome doctor hubby like, well, an elegant new nose.

Doctor Prassad Panaik took my extended hand in both of his, squeezed it a tad too warmly, and offered me what I believe he thought was an intimate wink. I felt a little rush of worry about the security of my old friend's marital accomplishment, but Sylvie stood there beaming. She said they had to rush off to a dinner party, but we should get together soon. Then she presented me with her business card: DR. SYLVIA KAHN, SEX

THERAPIST. By the time I read these words, the Doctors Panaik and Kahn were gone.

Happily, the following week when we met for lunch, I discovered that Sylvie's wit had not altered as much as the rest of her had. Telling me one story, she even performed an impish parody of her husband, complete with New Delhi accent and gooey-eyed wink. Of course, I was dying to know how she had gotten into the sex therapy biz and Sylvie willingly obliged.

She told me she had been working on her Ph.D. in art history at NYU when she met Prassad, a urologist at Saint Vincent's Hospital. At about the same time that they decided to get married, she realized if she had to write another sentence in "art-speak," she would die of terminal hypocrisy. Trouble was, she wasn't qualified to do anything else. It was Prassad who suggested a new career; he said every hospital and clinic in the city was suddenly desperate to put a sex therapist on staff, but the supply was severely limited. Even more helpfully, Prassad told her he could obtain a doctorate in psychology for her by mail from a "very respected" university in his homeland. That, plus a three-week course at the Masters and Johnson clinic in Saint Louis, would qualify her to work anywhere she wanted.

At first, it was the hoax quotient of the whole deal that appealed to Sylvie. "After all those years of academic bullshit, becoming a *genuine* fraud seemed positively refreshing," she said. But after only one week at the Saint Louis clinic, she experienced an epiphany: She possessed a natural gift for dispensing sex therapy.

"Try and figure," Sylvia said to me. "Scratch the cynic and you find a Samaritan." That was my first hint that my old friend, Sylvia, believed she was answering a higher calling.

A few lunches later, Sylvie told me about sex surrogates. At the time, I was still cheerfully climbing the corporate ladder at that food conglomerate where I was pulling in six figures, so the idea of switching professions could not have been farther from my mind. But that didn't mean I wasn't fascinated. I had to know absolutely everything. How much did it pay? (Between $300 and $700 per session.) What exactly did these surrogates do at these sessions? (They taught the patients "sensual touch and response," then, at the appropriate moment, they initiated "sexual relations" with them.) Where did they see the patients? How often? And most intriguingly of all, "Where in the world do you *find* the women to do this, Sylvie?"

"Mostly at graduate schools," Sylvie answered. "Columbia, Fordham, Julliard. Especially Julliard. Financial aid is notoriously stingy over there. And actually, an artistic temperament makes the job a lot easier." I can still laugh myself silly recalling that line about artistic temperament. But to tell the truth, I wasn't surprised by any of it. When Sylvie and I were in college, the Providence vice squad broke up a coed call-girl ring at Brown. As I recall, one of the girls was quoted in the press as saying, "All the other girls here are giving it away free. If there's one thing I learned in Economics 101, it's that there's a slim profit margin in free goods."

"But how do you recruit them?" I asked Sylvia.

"I put an ad in the college newspaper," she said. "You know, one of those, 'Students needed for psychological experiment' things. I say that it pays exceedingly well and the response is huge. I interview them in my office, so the sign on my door already tells them it's got something to do with sex therapy. And when I get around to the nitty-gritty of the job description, nine out of ten of them just nod and say, 'So how much does it pay?'"

"Incredible."

"Not really," Sylvie said. "I get to know these girls pretty well and most of them have done their fair share of joyless fucking. Usually with boyfriends they don't care about that much. Or with some guy who picks them up. So in a way, this amounts to an improvement. I've got one who only had one sexual experience before taking the job. She's a violist from Oklahoma and she says she doesn't have time for a real relationship in her life right now, so this is perfect for her."

"We live in liberated times," I said.

"Not really," Sylvie replied seriously. "Maybe people are screwing more, but they are enjoying it less. That's why I have a waiting list that's a mile long."

"Most of your patients are married, right?"

Sylvie nodded.

"So why don't they practice that touchy-feely thing with each other? Instead of with a stranger?"

"Basically, because they bring too much baggage into bed with them. Stuff about money, the children, the in-laws. Insults and slights, old and new. Who took out the garbage last. You name it. It all makes it virtually impossible for them to be tender with each other. So we have to work backwards— jump-start their sensuality with a baggage-free surrogate.

Among other things, it makes these men remember what they've been missing. And once they get the hang of it again, they want to bring it back home."

It all sounded so sensible to me at the time. Even that business about sensually reawakened men wanting to bring it all back home. I have always favored a practical, no-nonsense approach to psychological problems. To me, coming to terms with my "superego" never seemed any more promising than coming to terms with the Holy Ghost. (And that's not all those two have in common.) In fact, the only part that puzzled me as we sat there eating moussaka, was how my old college buddy could talk about it so earnestly. So *double entendre*–free. Had Sylvia matured faster than I had?

It was near the end of this memorable luncheon when Sylvie mentioned ever-so-casually that for some of her patients, an older surrogate would be more appropriate, especially for those who have daughters in graduate school. Fast forward two-plus years and there Sylvie and I are again, having our monthly lunch together, but this time yours truly is jobless, job-prospectless, and living on Frank Macy's generous, but limited, monthly stipend. I had recently picked up my very own copy of *Diaries of a Venetian Courtesan* at the Strand, and every entry I read put a smile on my lips and a song in my heart (say, Violetta's aria to sexual freedom in *La Traviata*). I asked Sylvie if she was still in the market for older surrogates, and without batting a false eyelash, she immediately scheduled me for a session with a distinguished old gentleman who hadn't made love to his wife in three years: Abe Levanthal.

The cabbie got me to Sylvie's building in record time.
In the elevator, I checked my watch: ten minutes to three. Good.
I took a deep breath and started to review what I might say to
her. Should I start right off by telling her I knew that Angelica
Linscott was one of her patients? Or should I save that until I
found out just how much Sylvie was ready to tell me on her
own? As I considered these alternatives, I glanced at the *New
York Post* that the elevator man had draped over the rail next to
him. All that was visible was the bottom half of the front page;
in its left corner was a boxed insert photo of a classy-looking
dame in a skirt suit. I leaned down to take a better look.

I was that classy-looking dame.

*Damn, I look good! The suit, the pumps, the turn of my calf, the
haughty-yet-beguiling tilt of my head.*

This thought lasted no more than a fraction of a second (or
however long it takes for the central nervous system to click
on the floodlights of context and memory). Then I felt my pho-
togenic knees buckle. *The shit has made contact with the fan.*

I grabbed the newspaper and held it in front of me. The
seventy-two-point bold headline was succinct: ICED! The full-
page photo was of Michael flat out on my bed with a hyper-
illuminated ice pick sticking out of his spine. Clearly, the photo
had been taken under the tungsten lamps of the NYPD's forensics department; it was undoubtedly their very own crime scene
photograph that some enterprising policeperson had sold to
the *Post* for enough cash, say, to purchase that lovely little pre-
fab sun room she'd always wanted. The little boxed photo of

me was from Saks Fifth Avenue. It had its own headline: SHOPS
UNTIL SHE DROPS FULL STORY: PAGE 2.

I turned to page two:

> Michael Linscott, a senior executive at First Boston
> Bank, was found murdered last night in the Fifth
> Avenue duplex bedroom of his paramour, Lydia
> Quess, a former senior executive at . . .

Well, how about that! The story was being spun as *Pecca-
dillos of the rich and famous,* not *John whacked in whore's boudoir.*
I was being portrayed as neither a call girl nor a sex surrogate,
but as a lady power broker. That was going to make the Widow
Linscott happy. I felt a little surge of relief myself. What can I
say? Bourgeois values die hard. It even occurred to me that the
Post's take belied a certain feminist perspective: *See? Women
power brokers can be just as despicable as male power brokers. We've
come a long way, Baby.* But of course, the *Post's* spin was targeted
to their prime demographic, working stiffs, and it recycled their
tried-and-true theme: The high and mighty are actually much
worse off than you are, friend. Like dead, for example.

The elevator had stopped at the seventh floor, where the
elevator man courteously waited for me to finish reading his
newspaper before opening the door. I began to read the next
paragraph:

> Ms. Quess, who resigned a few years ago from the
> Fortune 500 company under a cloud of accusa-
> tions of questionable accounting practices, has

not yet been arrested. After spending last night
in a suite at the Sherry-Netherland Hotel, she
went on a shopping spree this morning at Saks
Fifth Avenue, where she made purchases totaling
$3,125 . . .

Questionable accounting practices? Utter bullshit, every
word of it!

Somebody buzzed the elevator. The elevator operator
reached for the lever that opened the door. I quickly skipped
down a few paragraphs:

A Wall Street analyst informed our reporter that
in 1999, this company was accused of submit-
ting false revenue reports in a $15 million loan
application. The dispute was settled out of court.
Ms. Quess's resignation was accepted soon afterward . . .

Unbelievable! They were making it up as they went along.
The *Post*'s spin was about something even sexier than sex:
Money. Corporate money. Loads of it. But the subtext was the
same as if it were a crime of passion: This was a revenge murder. A multimillion-dollar revenge murder. And former senior
vice president, Lydia Quess, a shopaholic with a serious business ethics problem, was obviously the murderer.

Another buzz. The elevator operator opened the door. I
reached into my pocketbook, fished out a five-dollar bill, and
handed it to him.

"For the newspaper," I said, stepping into the hallway. Now I only had to buy up a million more copies and nobody would ever see it.

I stuffed the paper into my bag and made for the office of Dr. Sylvia Kahn, Ph.D. (New Delhi Technical Institute). A dour-looking couple in their forties was seated next to one another in the waiting room, each reading a magazine (she, *People*; he, *Simple Life*). Only the woman looked up when I made my entrance. I nodded to her and strode to Sylvie's office door, gave a quick knock, and entered.

"What are you doing here?" Sylvie snapped. I had caught the five-minutes-to window—nobody else was in there. Sylvia was munching on an Ensure low-fat energy bar at her desk. "Close the door!"

I closed the door behind me.

"You were right about having to be careful," I said to Sylvie. "I'm a suspect, all right. And it's already in the papers."

"So I heard," Sylvie said. She gestured for me to sit down in the patient chair opposite hers. The power arrangement was clear: She was in the therapeutic catbird seat.

"I need to ask you about Angelica Linscott. I had lunch with her today," I said.

Sylvia set down her own half-eaten lunch. Apparently, she had just lost her low-fat appetite. "What did she say?"

"She said she wanted me to talk to you about keeping her own sex therapy on the Q.T.," I said. "But I'm not sure if that is really in my best interest. Or yours either. Not to mention that it wouldn't be the ethical thing to do."

"Oh, *ethics*! My favorite subject," Sylvia answered, her voice dripping with icy sarcasm. The sarcasm had not changed from our Barnard days, but the iciness had multiplied exponentially.

"You never told me you employed male sex surrogates," I said.

"*That* would have been unethical," Sylvie retorted. "It's none of your business."

"Are you going to tell the police about Angelica's therapy?"

"That's none of your business either, Lydia."

"I suppose not," I said. "But if you didn't tell them and I did, that might seem odd to them, to say the least."

That was a threat coming out of my mouth. And I have to say that it surprised me as much as it did Sylvia; I hadn't planned a word of it. Nonetheless, it felt exactly like what the occasion demanded.

"What is it you want, Lydia?" Sylvia said.

Sylvie *did* have the instincts of a therapist: She immediately reduced the situation at hand to a question of basic desire. Good question. I knew the answer.

"I want the name of the surrogate Mrs. Linscott was seeing," I said. "Is *still* seeing, actually."

Sylvia suddenly reached for her diet bar, but I knew it was just a cover move. And it didn't begin to cover what I believe it was supposed to: Sylvia had not known that Angelica Linscott was still seeing her surrogate lover. Among other things, that meant that Dr. Kahn, Ph.D., had not been getting her twenty-five percent referral fees. That, by the way, made this surrogate different from me: I continued to give Sylvia her cut long after her patients had completely mastered the technique of "sensual touch and response." It was simply the right thing to do.

"Give you his name," Sylvia repeated slowly. "And then you won't tell the police anything about Mrs. Linscott's association with me?"

"Exactly," I said. At the moment, I meant it.

"That might be a breach of professional ethics," Sylvie announced finally. "I'll have to think about this and get back to you, Lydia."

That term, "professional ethics," had acquired a special meaning for me during the Formula Fiasco. It turns out to be a synonym for "looking impeccable while screwing the competition." I was weighing the profitability of pointing this out to Sylvie when who should come strolling out of her office bathroom but Doctor Prassad Panaik, who had apparently interrupted his afternoon application of hair mousse to join our conversation.

"We'll give you his name on three conditions," Prassad said, stopping directly in front of me. "First, you do not reveal to him or anyone else where you got it from. And second, you assure us absolutely that you will not reveal Angelica's professional association with Sylvia to the authorities."

Sylvie nervously stuffed the remainder of her Ensure bar into her mouth. She seemed surprised that her husband was being so forthcoming with me. She also appeared somewhat unsettled by the way he referred to Mrs. Linscott by her first name.

"I believe you have agreed to that already," Prassad went on, "but I wanted to stress that there could be serious repercussions for you, too, if you did this."

Well done, Doctor: You threaten me, I threaten you. It's the great American way. Dr. Panaik was obviously an expert on professional ethics.

"And the third condition?" I asked.

Sylvie's husband worked up his gooey-eyed thing before answering, "I want you to be very careful with him, Lydia. I believe he has some control problems."

"In bed?" I said. I couldn't help myself.

"I'm serious, Lydia," the good doctor said waspishly.

"Yes, I'm sorry. I appreciate your warning and promise you everything," I said. "I'm just a little on edge today."

"That's understandable," Prassad said. "His name is Danny Bloomster, and he's at 185 Sullivan Street."

"My neighborhood."

Sylvia stood. "I have patients waiting," she said.

As I was stepping into the hallway, I heard Sylvia apologize to the couple who had been kept waiting. "Please come in," she was saying blithely as the door closed. "This isn't going to hurt a bit."

When the elevator arrived to pick me up, the operator gave me a big grin of recognition. I assumed it was because of the five bucks I had recently laid on him, but then I saw that he had a brand new copy of the *Post* tucked under his arm and there I was again, beaming boldly just below the fold. So the elevator operator had figured out that he had a personal relationship with a celebrity murder suspect. Clearly, I needed to change my clothes again ASAP. I am decent looking, but hardly a head turner, especially in New York, the Mecca for top beauties. That is, except on those rare occasions when I step out wearing designer clothes. *Then* heads turn. There is a reason why Rena Lange suits cost so much: They make an impression. In order to return to my natural low visibility, I needed to dress down.

Head tucked, I ambled over to Morris Brothers' Sporting Goods on Broadway. There, I went on another shopping spree, this one to the tune of $77.85 for a long-sleeved T-shirt emblazoned with the words JUST DO IT!, sweatpants, and slip-on Keds. I emerged from Morris Brothers' looking like a nanny from some small middle-European principality, complete with a plastic bag containing my Rena Lange suit dangling from my wrist. Nobody so much as glanced at me.

I opted for a cab to get back downtown instead of an IRTful of loyal *New York Post* readers.

Paddy had been right, there was information Sylvia—
and her husband—could tell me that they would not volun-
teer to the police. Why didn't they want the police to know
about Angelica Linscott's hands-on therapy? Ultimately, I figured, because it would lead to bad publicity. There was apparently something particularly lewd (not to mention juicy)
about a male sex surrogate, something, say, that the *New York
Post* could have a field day exploiting. Likely they hoped the
murder would be solved before anybody else had to know
about the ins and outs of modern sex therapy in The Big Apple.

Paddy and Abe had been right about something else too:
Captain Liu notwithstanding, it would be naive to leave it entirely up to the NYPD to prove my innocence. I needed to do
some supplementary snooping of my own. Angelica's lover was
high on my personal suspect list, and now I had his name and

address. The cabbie let me out across from the Sullivan Street Theater, late of the long-running *Fantasticks'* fame, now in the process of being renovated for high-income housing. Soon nobody would even try to remember what used to be there.

Danny Bloomster's name was one of six posted on the door of 185 Sullivan Street, a lovely old, red-brick, Greenwich Village original, but there was only one buzzer. I rang the bell before giving myself a chance to think about what I was going to say. No response. I rang again. Finally the front door was opened by a tall, remarkably handsome man with short brown hair. He was wearing a black silk shirt and *gray, pin-striped pants.* At that moment, there was not a doubt in my mind that the intrepid Ms. Quess had solved the murder mystery on the spot. *Close-cropped brown hair, gray pin-striped trousers*—zipiddy-dippidy, case closed.

"Mr. Bloomster?" I said.

"Hardly." Only two syllables, but more than sufficient to inform me he was gay.

Damn, not solved. "Is he in?" I asked.

"He's working."

"So he's home." I figured Bloomster worked at home like I did.

"No," he said. Pin-stripe gave me a bored look and began to close the door. "He's at what's-his-face's bar."

"Where is that?"

"I don't know. Around the corner."

With that, he shut the door in my face.

I walked to the end of the block and turned the corner. In three steps, I was standing under a neon sign that read

MORGAN'S BAR AND GRILLE. I immediately recognized Danny Bloomster through the window. Let me explain:

On the same day that I signed on with Sylvia Kahn, a courier arrived at my building with a discreet little package. Agron brought it up to me. It was a video entitled *Learning to Love Again,* produced and distributed, the label said, by The Kahn-Panaik Institute. A Post-it attached to the cassette said, "Lydia, F.Y.I. Touch and response exercises. Study carefully. Sylvie." I poured myself a juice-glassful of pinot grigio and slipped the tape into my VCR.

If someone had told me that *Learning to Love Again* was a MAD-TV production, I would have fired off a fan letter immediately, although I would have suggested that a better title would be *The* Job *of Sex.* It was fall-off-the-couch hilarious, a tongue-in-cheek riff on self-conscious, sex-manual sex. Except, of course, it was utterly sincere. While Sylvia's saccharine voice-over said things like, "Very gently touch the inside of your partner's thighs with your fingertips" and "Focus on your senses," a naked young man and a naked young woman dutifully acted out her instructions on top of a brightly lit four-poster. There were nice production values in the bed and linen department—straight out of Pottery Barn. But although both participants smiled enthusiastically for the entire half hour, the effect was anything but erotic. They made sex look like Pilates exercises.

Now fully clothed in a Grateful Dead T-shirt and jeans, the male lead of *Learning to Love Again* was serving drinks from behind the bar of Morgan's Bar and Grille. It had to be Danny Bloomster. I walked in and ordered a champagne cocktail.

Bloomster was about my age, sandy-haired, shortish, loose-limbed, and rather ordinary-looking except for his eyes, which were deep-set, bright blue, and highly animated. "Dramatic" would probably be a better word. Like nine out of ten New York bartenders, Danny Bloomster was obviously biding his time until that fateful audition that would change his life (not to mention the entire history of theater) forever after. If I had not deduced that from his over-the-top eye technique, I would have from his voice when he repeated my order. He gave "champagne cocktail" a decidedly quirky, Al Pacino–esque reading.

As Bloomster sidled over to the fridge under the bar, I tried to envision how Angelica Linscott perceived him. I had no idea how intelligent or articulate Bloomster was, but in any event, it would have been difficult to outshine Michael in that department. Yet what was *not* hard to imagine was how Bloomster's downtown, art-for-art's-sake *mise-en-scène* contrasted with life in the 'burbs, even if Sullivan Street had become a high-rent district. Whenever the Met is strapped for cash, they trot out another Zeffirelli production of *La Bohème,* complete with three-hundred-and-fifty-dollar orchestra seats; suffering-for-art enthralls the imaginations of ladies who can afford those seats. I could picture Bloomster's apartment, the Klimt poster on the bare brick wall, Leonard Cohen whimpering on the CD player, overdue library books stacked precariously by the side of the unmade bed. But of course, it was what Bloomster brought into that bed that ultimately counted, his well-toned young body—no number of trips to the New York Athletic Club could have given Michael a body like that.

Bloomster returned with my drink.

"I feel like I've seen you someplace," I said. "The theater. A movie. I can't place it."

Bloomster's bright eyes did a little dance.

"I'm currently in a revival of *The Indian Wants the Bronx*," he said. "Over at The Loft Playhouse. I'm artistic director there."

Of course! Bloomster's vocalizing *was* pure Pacino. I half expected him to snarl, "*Hey, Pussyface!*"

"No, I haven't seen that yet," I said. I took a deliberate, Actor's Studio sip of my champagne before continuing. "Oh, I remember. It *was* a movie. *Learning to Love Again*."

Instantly, Bloomster's eyes turned cold. Very expressive, those eyes of his.

"My early work," Bloomster said archly. "I like to think of it as a romantic comedy."

"I got the comedy part," I said.

Bloomster planted both his elbows on the bar, cupped his jaw in his hands, and leaned in toward me. "Of course, the question is, lady, what were you doing in the audience?"

"Homework," I said. "I needed a little brushup on my touch and response exercises."

Bloomster's laugh was both theatrical and unpleasant. "And now you and your hubby are getting it on again. I am *so* glad I could be of service."

"I'm afraid it didn't work," I improvised. "He touched, but I didn't respond."

Bloomster leaned in even closer. "I get the feeling you knew you'd find me here," he said.

"That's right."

"Who told you?"

"Angelica. Angelica Linscott."

Bloomster's eyes told the truth again: He was stunned. He straightened up, turned his back to me, then swung back holding a glassful of Scotch. He took a long draw on it before he spoke.

"How do you know Angelica?"

"We go way back," I said. "Prep school and beyond."

Bloomster studied my face, then my JUST DO IT! T-shirt. It would have been a lot easier to pull off my newly adopted role if I'd still been dressed by Saks. "I had lunch with Angelica today," I continued. "She's bearing up surprisingly well."

"Glad to hear that," Bloomster said in a slightly bored voice.

Another patron—a long-haired young man in paint-splattered overalls—approached the bar and Bloomster immediately scurried over to take his order. If Danny Bloomster had anything to do with Michael's murder, I couldn't tell by his reactions. In fact, I couldn't even be sure he *knew* that Angelica's husband was dead. The only shock he'd registered was when I said Angelica had pointed me in his direction. And that shock could have been about any number of things. I drank down my champagne cocktail.

"What's your pleasure, ma'am?" Bloomster said when he returned, eyeing my empty glass.

"That's what I'd like to know," I replied. "My pleasure's been in short supply lately."

"I guess we ought to do something about that, shouldn't we?" Bloomster said.

"I guess we should," I said. *Ugh.*

"I'm free tonight after the show," Bloomster said. "We could meet here at—let's say, eleven."

"Tonight?"

"Otherwise, I'm pretty much booked."

"I could manage to get out then," I said. This felt weird. *Very* weird. "There's no need to involve Dr. Kahn, is there?" I said.

"No."

"Then—?" I looked down bashfully, no method acting required.

"Five hundred," Bloomster replied. "Cash, of course."

"See ya later," I said, and I got out of there as fast as I could.

9

There was no way in hell that I would have sex with Danny Bloomster. Not even if it meant I would miss out on uncovering important evidence. I would rather spend the rest of my life in prison. This had nothing to do with my fine-tuned sense of morality. It had everything to do with the self-satisfied smirk on Danny Bloomster's face.

Without thinking, I made my way to Washington Square Park and was now passing under the glorious Stanford White Arch at the north end. I read that in 1890-something, when workmen dug down to sink the cornerstone of this arch, they uncovered human bones. Apparently the park had once been the final destination of New York's paupers, a potter's field just a stone's throw away from the stately homes of the Jamesian set. I like to think of the great white arch as a memorial to those anonymous people. Heaven knows, George Washington has enough things named after him.

I was just a half a block away from my apartment. Habit, I guess, like a dog whose owner moves to the other side of town but who keeps nosing his way back to his old home. I could see Agron in his gray, military-looking uniform toting a garbage bag to one of the cans by the curb. I headed straight for him.

"Hi. Remember me?" I said.

Agron turned around. Although he is a big man to begin with, his head is two sizes too large for the rest of him, and this makes him look like a David Levine caricature. That and the fact that every feature on his long face slants downward from the center. It is a touching face. Agron placed a hand on each of my shoulders.

"I never forget you, Mrs. Quess. In this life or next one," he said.

Back in Kosovo, he had been raised a Muslim; now he reads New Age spirit and angel books in every spare moment.

"That's good to hear," I said.

Agron peered into the apartment building to see if anyone needed him, then leaned down and whispered, "Police lady up there again."

"Well, I sure hope she finds something," I said.

Agron looked surprised. Did that mean he thought I had something to hide?

"No job for a lady," Agron said, nodding his head somberly.

"What job is that?" Although I trusted Agron, I had taken pains to keep him in the dark about my line of work. I'd figured it might suffer in cultural translation.

"Homicide," Agron said. "You need to think like man to catch killer."

"Really? What if the killer is a woman?" *That* was the wrong thing to say. What did I think I was doing—making a feminist point?

"I stick up for you no matter how people talk," Agron said.

"What people? And how do they talk?"

"People in building. People that see your picture in the newspaper."

No doubt the neighborhood kiosk had sold out the early afternoon edition of the *Post* in record time.

"I'm sure they're unhappy with the publicity," I said.

"They do not want you to live here anymore," Agron said dejectedly.

"Oh." That was no surprise. My building is teeming with graying veterans of picket lines and the Summer of Love who, with the aid of modern reproductive technology, have produced a generation of smug-looking little boys and girls who look to be their grandchildren and go to private schools where they learn Native American dances in gym class. Most of these people drive Volvos, carefully leaving the mud splatters from their weekends in the Berkshires on the windshields. The tenants committee had recently taken to issuing Big Brother proclamations against foul language and "inappropriate" dress in the vestibule and corridors. I could hardly expect them to be concerned about my civil rights.

"The people stink," Agron said.

"All the way to the afterlife," I said.

"Your friend, the dead man, he had many foes, did he not?"

"What makes you say that?"

"I see him sometime at the Yale Club," Agron said. "He fights with people there. Sometimes Bruno must ask him to volume down."

Agron works as a runner in the Yale Club's Roof Dining Room three nights a week. He once told me the place reminds him of a bazaar back in Prizren—little groups of bald-headed men whispering and haggling. This was the first time he ever mentioned seeing Michael Linscott there. For that matter, it was the first time he ever mentioned anything to me about any of my weekly visitors.

"What kind of fights? In the gym?"

"In the dining room," Agron answered. "Word fights. Pounding on the table fights."

That was certainly a side of Michael I was unaware of. I always pictured him as one of those patrician bankers who got his way simply by displaying his perfect teeth.

"Business people carrying long pieces of paper. Making deals, as you say. Mr. Linscott keeps a room at the club for business."

Michael had a personal room at the Yale Club? I bet Angelica didn't know about it either. Well, well, had Michael been using it for assignations with other women? It *was* a gentleman's hobby, after all.

I was about to ask Agron if he recognized any of the business types with whom Michael had fought, when I saw Captain Amy Liu coming out the front door of my building.

"Ms. Quess," she said, nodding. "Afraid we've still got some work to do up there."

"I was just in the neighborhood," I said. Not exactly a brilliant rejoinder; it sounded like some kind of lame alibi.

Liu nodded again and started to cross the street. I immediately followed, falling in beside her.

"Did you see the *Post*?" I said.

"Yes."

"None of it is true, you know," I said. "I didn't resign because of questionable accounting practices. I resigned because—"

"I know why you resigned, Ms. Quess," Liu said, not looking at me.

"How?"

"I do my homework," she said. I thought I detected the hint of a smile of approval for my *chutzpa* in taking on a corporate giant. Of course, at this point in the day, I was ready to see a heartening sign in just about anything. "So, how's the investigation going?" I said, trying to sound breezy.

"Smoothly," Liu replied, effortlessly out-breezing me.

We reached a 1995 Ford Escort parked next to a fire hydrant. A well-worn placard leaning against the inside of the windshield read, NYPD OFFICIAL BUSINESS. Captain Liu finally turned to face me.

"Listen, Ms. Quess, I was going to call you, but I might as well take care of this piece of business now," she said.

The ominous way she delivered this line made every vital organ in my body cringe. Take care of *what*, exactly? *Measuring my neck for the noose?*

"Your saliva was accidentally contaminated in the forensics lab," Captain Liu went on. "They need another for your DNA profile."

Relieved, I laughed. I saw Liu coolly studying my face. Maybe Abe was right, I *did* have a death wish. Heaven knows, I definitely had a penchant for inappropriate responses in front of the murder investigators.

I was saved by an electronic beep: Liu's cell phone rang in her pocket. She removed it, turned her back to me, and had a hushed and economical conversation. When she was finished, she shoved the phone into her pocket and faced me again. For a moment, she was silent, apparently debating something in her mind; then she said, "I have to return to my office. Forensics is over there too. I could give you a lift, if you want to take care of that saliva business now."

"I don't have anything else scheduled," I said.

Liu opened the passenger door of her car and I got in. Other than a police radio haphazardly fastened to the underside of the dashboard and one of those magnetized blue dome lights that can be popped on the car roof, the interior of Liu's station wagon looked like that of any outer-borough, just-making-ends-meet family: baby seat strapped down just behind the driver; deflated volleyball; a couple of empty cans of Heineken; several Whopper wrappers. Liu drove several blocks north, eyes straight ahead, without saying a word. I had been hoping for a little conversation.

"So, how're the kids?" I said finally. It wasn't meant to be flippant. Honestly.

"You understand that this is an irregular procedure," Liu replied.

"Talking about your children?"

"No, giving you a lift."

"Well, thanks, I guess."

"That does not mean that anything you say in here may not be held against you," Liu said, clearly in full control of her double negatives.

"Fine with me," I said. "So for the record, I didn't kill Michael Linscott."

"That statement is already on the record," Liu said.

"Just making sure."

"Incidentally, I only have one child," Liu said.

"That's infinitely more than I have."

"To your infinite regret?"

"Babies are still an option," I said. "But I'm hoping to mature a bit before I get started."

Liu granted me a guarded smile.

At Union Square, she turned onto Park Avenue South, then took the scenic route around Gramercy Park, passing by Raphael's duplex on our left. Obviously, this was not a coincidence; I'd given Liu his address.

"Your Señor Llargos has not been returning our calls or answering his door," she said.

"He travels a lot."

"What kind of business is he in?"

"He's what the French call a *fils à papa*," I said. I was prepared to translate—that Raphael lived off his rich and disapproving father—but Liu's nod made that unnecessary.

We parked in front of an antique, red stone building on Twenty-First Street, a precinct house from the *Naked City* era, but Liu led me around the corner to a sixties-modern, brick monstrosity attached to it at the rear. Over the door, a metal sign read DETECTIVE BOROUGH MANHATTAN. My freshman comp instructor would have had some serious issues with that sequence of words: "Is that his first name—*Borough?* Well, it certainly does sound Irish."

Captain Liu rapidly tapped the combination into the front door lock, then signaled me to precede her in. We took an elevator to the fifth floor, where she dropped me off in the forensics lab waiting room.

"We'll be talking," she said perfunctorily, and started to leave.

"Should I look for you on my way out?" I asked.

"I'll probably be gone," she said, and she was gone.

This time, instead of a diminutive forensics cop, a female lab assistant in an extra-large white coat scooped out my saliva. She dropped my swab into a test tube and sealed it.

"Don't spit in my saliva this time," I said with a nervous laugh. I am in the habit of making dumb jokes when faced with white-coated authority figures.

She gave me a withering look.

I was on the ground floor, heading for the exit with my Morris Brothers' bag swinging at my side, when I spotted Amy Liu through a half-open office door to my right. She was standing alone in front of a bulletin board on wheels that was covered with photographs. From a distance, they looked like stills from *The Texas Chainsaw Massacre.* I went over to the office door and peered in.

Left to right, high-gloss digital photographs were lined up like a storyboard, starting with the teaser, vivid shots of walls, carpet, and bed in a small, windowless room. Blood covered everything. There was more of it than I thought any single human could contain. Or leak.

The next row of photographs featured the victim—a brown-skinned woman who lay face up, her torso on the bed, her legs dangling off its side. She could have been twenty years old at the most. My guts began churning. Even if these were only photographs, this was the second dead body I'd seen in twenty-four hours.

"Babycakes." Captain Liu was looking at me.

"Beg pardon?"

"That was her street name," Liu said.

I took this as permission to enter, which I did. "Murdered?"

"Beaten to death," Liu said. "A bullet between the eyes would have been more merciful."

"My God."

"Four hours ago Babycakes was eating a blueberry Pop-Tart," Liu said. "They found the wrapper on the floor, blueberries in her teeth—what were left of them."

"She was a prostitute?" I said.

"From the Lincoln Tunnel brigade. They're known as 'last chance' girls. They hang out near the tunnel entrance, and their clientele are New Jersey–bound executives who struck out in the singles bars. It's a dependable john pool."

"Any witnesses?"

"Barely one."

"Incompetent?"

"Somewhere between incompetent and uncooperative," Liu said. "She was murdered in a by-the-hour hotel room.

Pay as you go. So the last person to see her alive was the desk clerk."

"So he must have seen the john she went up with," I said.

"Alertness is not a job requirement for a desk clerk in an SRO hotel. But when pressed, he did admit to hearing a few screams upstairs around the time of the murder."

The hint of a smirk appeared on Captain Liu's lips when she used the word "pressed," which made me believe she meant it literally: She had *pressed* the desk clerk forcefully against the grungy walls of the hotel lobby, probably with the aid of a police baton pressed against his Adam's apple. It was a disquieting image, but thrilling nonetheless. Amy Liu is my height—five-seven—and cannot possibly weigh more than a hundred and twenty pounds, but there is a virtuosity to her movements that would make any man think twice about fighting back.

"So he heard screams, but he didn't go upstairs to see where they came from?" I said.

"That's about it," Liu said with a sigh. I got the distinct impression she had already told me more than she had intended to.

"Didn't you ask him why he didn't run upstairs immediately when he heard her screaming?"

"Of course."

"And?"

"None of this is remotely relevant to your situation, Ms. Quess," Liu said coolly.

"Perhaps I can offer you some professional perspective," I said.

"Maybe you can at that," Liu said. No sooner had she said this than she removed a notebook from her back pocket and flipped through a few pages before stopping. Then she began to read her notes out loud to me. It was a dramatic reading, replete with a droll impression of the dull-witted witness.

"'What did you hear?'

"'I dunno, maybe a little yelling or something. But a lot of them make noise, ya know? That's part of the show. These guys can have a silent fuck at home with the old lady. Here, they want some fireworks.'"

An explanation Sylvia Kahn might offer to explain why a surrogate was better equipped than the spouse for jump-starting a nonperforming husband's snoozing sensuality. In slightly different words, of course.

"'What kind of fireworks?'" Liu continued reading.

"'Moaning, groaning, grunting, wailing. You know—sound effects.'

"'How about, screaming for help? Is that a sound effect you hear often?'

"'More often than you'd think, lady.'

"'And you just sat there.'

"'I mind my own business, if that's what you mean. Anyways, leaving my post is against regulations.'"

Liu closed her notebook. "Fortunately," she said, "he did give me a pretty good description of Babycakes's pimp and her coworkers after I pressed him a bit further."

"I hope you didn't leave any marks on his body," I said.

"Not so you'd notice," she replied, deadpan. She started for the door. "I have to leave now. Can I drop you somewhere?"

"Where are you going?" I asked.

"Home."

"Where's that?"

"Doesn't matter. I can drop you wherever you want."

The truth is, I wanted to go home with Amy Liu. I wanted to see her apartment, meet her kid, and whoever it was in her household who drank Heineken beer with her. In fact, at that particular moment, sight-unseen, I wanted to move in with the whole bunch of them. I was in serious need of a surrogate family.

"Grand Central Station," I said.

Liu eyed me skeptically. "We still require you to stay in town, you know."

"I like the food court there," I lied.

Back in the car, I asked, "Will you catch him? The man who murdered Babycakes?"

"Fifty-fifty, maybe less," Liu said. "The perp is not an intimate partner or family member. So the percentages start dropping right there. On the other hand, I'm sure forensics will be able to lift good prints and tissue samples. All those kicks and punches were not premeditated, so I doubt he brought along rubber gloves. But finding a match is always chancy. I'm sure Babycakes had a big turnover of customers. Probably not that many repeats, either."

"What makes you think that?"

"Her territory," Liu said. "Lincoln Tunnel johns are looking for something strange. Not steady companionship."

"Unlike mine," I said.

Liu did not react to that. "I have a specific allocation for this type of homicide," she went on. "One week and we file it under cold cases."

"You're kidding me."

"No, Ms. Quess, not kidding. We have limited resources. I have a whole book full of tables and graphs that calculate by category the probability of making a case. If it looks like the husband or wife or son or daughter is the perp, that gets the highest priority. More resources, more time."

"Because you're more likely to find them?"

"That's right."

"There's something backwards about that, isn't there?" I said. "I mean, the harder the case is to solve, the less time it gets?"

"Like any business, we try to maximize our profits," Liu said. "We put our money where we think it's going to pay off."

So, at least part of Abe's dictum about how the NYPD operates was true. Liu stopped at the red light on Fifth Avenue, then turned right on Forty-Second Street. She turned her head toward me. "So, why do you suppose Babycakes was killed? You have any theories on her john's motives?"

Why did this feel like a test?

"Anger, fury?" I said.

"A crime of passion."

"I suppose. Funny word, 'passion.'"

"But anger about what?" Liu said. "Assuming they just met, what could that be?"

"Maybe something she said or did."

"For instance?"

"Something that struck him as humiliating. About the size of his organ maybe."

"I can't imagine any prostitute would go there. Unless she had a death wish," Liu said.

There seemed to be a lot of people talking about death wishes today.

"It's all in the interpretation," I said. "Selective perception. Say the girl says, 'It's a little dark in here.' All the john hears is the word 'little' and he goes ballistic."

"He's hypersensitive," Liu said with an ironic smile. The light had changed and she started the car moving again.

"Yes," I said. "And more than a little crazy too."

"Of course, maybe he has good reason for his sensitivity," Liu said. "Maybe he does have a tiny dick."

Was Amy Liu making a funny? I studied her face for a clue. None there.

"Well, I suppose you could use that as a working hypothesis," I said, deadpan. "Round up the usual tiny-dick suspects."

"Dick profiling?" Liu said. "That's against the law."

This time she couldn't keep her smile under control. I liked this woman. Whatever her test was, I wanted an A on it.

"Or maybe the whole deal is inside the john's head," I said. "Say, Babycakes reminds him of his mother. Maybe she was a working girl herself."

"How does that help the investigation?" Liu asked.

"Maybe he's done it before," I said. "Maybe he's roughed up some other working girl, and there's a record of it."

"Good," Liu said. "So we round those up. And then we do a lineup for the desk clerk and Babycakes's pimp and her pals."

"That sounds right."

"And that's exactly what we will do unless we come up with a positive ID from prints or from a witness before then."

"That's great," I said. I had a feeling that I was acing this quiz.

"I still give it fifty-fifty at best," Liu said. She pulled up across the street from Grand Central, threw the car into neutral, and turned in her seat to face me. "Some of the more experienced girls carry weapons with them for just such occasions. Small revolvers, knives. They keep them stashed under their wigs and then hide them under the mattress. I'd say once every four or five weeks we get a call about a john who's been maimed or murdered in self-defense. Judges are pretty good about dismissing cases like that. Unless the girl makes a habit of it. Too bad Babycakes wasn't one of those girls."

Shit.

This was the moment for me to say I killed Michael in self-defense.

Experienced hooker that I was, I hid a weapon (an ice pick!) under my mattress against the chance that one of my johns got rough. It was a standard risk of the job, so a girl had every right to be prudent. *That* was why Captain Liu had invited me in to chat about this case in the first place. A little jolt of shock therapy in the form of that bloody storyboard, then tease the hook into my mouth by making me beg for details, followed by a casual mention of my probable motive, and top it all off with the suggestion that I probably wouldn't even be prosecuted for it.

It hurt.

Not just that Amy Liu believed I was guilty, but that she had been playing me.

Even our little chortle about dick profiling was a calculated setup. Some girl "bonding" to gain my trust before she moved in for the kill. Damn it, just a few minutes ago I'd been willing to move in with her and her family, no questions asked. But Amy Liu was not looking for a friend. She had an entire family somewhere waiting for her to come home for dinner. I was the one who needed a friend. Captain Liu needed to wrap up a case.

"So tell me, Captain." I unlatched the car door and pushed it open. "Where does the Linscott case fall in your book of graphs? Does it qualify for more than a week before it gets filed away?"

"Absolutely," Liu said. "We have a special graph for victims with six-figure bank accounts."

I got out and slammed the door shut.

Ten minutes later, I emerged from a stall in the ladies' room of Grand Central Station, dressed to kill in my Rena Lange suit, silk stockings, and black pumps. It was cocktail hour at the Yale Club.

10

"Are you a member, madam?"

"No, I'm meeting a member for drinks," I said to the club concierge, a man who clearly had been chosen for the job on the basis of his supercilious tone of voice.

"And what would his name be?"

"I don't know what it would be, but it *is* Hartley. Joseph Hartley," I replied.

Hartley had occupied the office next to mine at my food corporation job; he wore his Yale tie every Friday prior to drinks at "The Club." When Agron mentioned that Michael maintained a private room at the Yale Club, I had been more than a little intrigued. What if he used it for other *liaisons*? A jealous mistress makes for a good murder suspect. And if this homicidal mistress were caught fast, who knows? She might get me off the front page of the *Post* and transform me into a sympathetic victim in my own right—the grieving *other* mistress.

As the concierge began to study his member list, I said jauntily, "I need to go to the little girls' room. Tell Joe I'll be right back." In a matter of seconds, I was in the stairwell, wending my way up to the fifth floor—the residency floor, according to a sign in the foyer.

There were only numbers on the residency room doors, no names. If the Yale Club administrators were aware of Michael's murder—as they surely must be—they had done nothing to cordon off his room, or do anything else that would call attention to it.

I stood, dumbly, in the middle of the hallway. *Very* dumbly. What the hell was I *doing* sneaking around in the Yale Club? I was a prime suspect in a murder! I should have told Captain Liu about the room and let her take it from there. It was not as if I didn't trust her to be thorough in her investigation. But did I trust her to be *timely*? What with Babycakes's murder, and who knows what else, by the time she got around to searching Michael's private room, somebody else could get in and muck up evidence. There was something else that propelled me to the fifth floor of the Yale Club, something none too rational: I wanted to prove myself to Amy Liu. Well, what I really wanted to do was one-up her.

A waiter exited one of the rooms walking backward, pulling a trolley out with him. He swung around and was now heading directly toward me. My line of work provides certain insights into male behavior and one pearl I've learned is that the status of a man's sexual pride determines just about everything he does. The waiter coming at me was surely no exception to this rule. He was in his mid-twenties, on the short side, but good-looking in a pubescent sort of way. He smiled at me.

I smiled back.

"Are you looking for something, miss?"

"Yes, Mr. Linscott's room."

If this waiter already knew about Michael's death, I had just screwed myself. And if he had seen the *Post,* he not only had seen my picture, but had seen my picture in this very outfit . . . however, the unruffled look on his face made me think I was in luck.

"I left my purse in there," I said.

The waiter and his trolley came to a full stop directly in front of me. I walked around beside him, then I placed one of my hands on the trolley handle next to his as a gesture of goodwill. Of course, he was free to interpret my gesture any way he wanted.

"I can probably put my hands on it in a minute," I said.

I smiled ambiguously, which in my case means lopsidedly.

The young waiter opened door number 7 with his passkey, let us both inside, and then closed the door behind us, leaving the trolley in the corridor.

First impression: If this room was Michael's idea of a romantic *boudoir,* I had failed miserably as his tutor. The place looked all business—*business* business. Two steel file cabinets in one corner, a desk by the window, computer, fax machine, phone and answering machine, even a paper shredder. The lone bed was narrow and antiseptic-looking. So much for my *other* other-woman scenario.

I could see that the file cabinets had some serious locks on them—Yale locks, no doubt—and that they were unlabeled. I walked over to the desk. Its top was bare but for three books: a hefty tome about business franchising law; *The Ultimate Corkscrew Book*; and a thin book titled *Red Lights Out: A Legal History of Disorderly Houses and Vice Districts, 1870–1917,* by one Thomas C. Mackey. *Curious.* Whatever business Michael had conducted here, it was not under the auspices of First Bank of Boston.

My eye caught on a small beribboned parcel under Michael's desk. The ribbons were red, but the wrapping was gray newsprint—*French* newsprint; *Livresse,* no doubt, the newspaper wrapper of choice in the book kiosks of Paris. All of the gift books Michael ever brought me from Paris had been done up like that. The package hardly seemed to be a clue—it looked like evidence of a trip to Paris, nothing more. However, it did qualify as portable.

"Here it is!" I chirped, stooping down to fetch the parcel.

My baby-faced waiter was giving me the fisheye. He knew damned well I was up to something that very closely resembled thievery. He took a tentative step toward the room's bed and smiled at me. Nothing particularly ambiguous about that smile.

There was a joke that went around Brooklyn in my teens: A boy asks a girl if she would sleep with him for a million bucks; she considers, and says, "Yes." The boy then asks, "How about for a dime?" The girl says, "What kind of girl do you take me for?" and the boy says, "We've already established that. Now we're just dickering over the price."

At the time, that joke struck me as high wit, sophisticated moral reasoning in a comic nutshell. But my career has forced me to inspect the logic of its underlying argument more closely. There are some men I would not even *consider* having sex with for a million dollars. Nonetheless, I do admit that if the price got up into that area, here and there I would probably modify my standards. All of which is to say that eager as I was to take that parcel with me, a quickie with this waiter was *not* a price I was willing to pay for it.

So I planted a luscious kiss on his lips and, parcel in hand, was out the door in a flash, calling over my shoulder, "I'd like to get to know you better, *much* better—soon, I hope."

If I was lucky, he would not come after me and relieve me of the parcel. Instead, those words would seal his loyalty and silence. Although he had not scored, he had achieved something even better—the *promise* of sex and a load of masturbatory hallucinations. I have found that in a man's mind future sex is usually more valuable than past sex. This is because future sex is more fertile material for fantasizing; with past sex, a man is stuck with the hard historical facts of a real encounter, always a serious limitation on his imagination. Men, it turns out, are far more romantic than we are; they are always dreaming of something better, sex that is sexier than sex itself.

I took the elevator down to the lobby. With a bit more luck, I would be out the front door before anyone else saw me.

But that was not to be the case. When the elevator doors separated, I stood face to face with one Roger Ricliffs, a member of the board of directors that had voted unanimously to terminate my employment in the middle of my whistle-blowing adventure. There was not a doubt in my mind that Ricliffs had seen the *Post* story. In fact, there was little doubt in my mind that he had had a hand in planting that bit about "a cloud of accusations of questionable accounting practices."

We stood there a long moment, me hiding my package behind my back, both of us playing chicken with our eyes. Finally Ricliffs said, "I certainly didn't expect to see you here, Ms. Quess."

"It's true," I replied. "I went to that other school. The one on the Charles, you know."

And I was out of there.

11

Sira wasn't home, but her harp was. It was by far the largest item in her compact, one-room apartment, dwarfing her spare, Swedish modern furnishings. She had left me a key with the doorman and a note taped to the scroll of her harp:

> *Lydia,*
>
> *So sorry about your situation. Make yourself at home.*
> *I'll stay at Jonah's. Keep in touch.*
>
> *Love, Sira*

I found something lacking in Sira's message, and especially in her absence. It wasn't just a place to sleep that I needed from my old friend. With a sigh, I phoned my apartment to check my answering machine. There were enough beeps for an entire Philip Glass symphony. Twelve of them turned out to be messages from reporters. Two of them, *The National Enquirer* and *Us,* were offering me "exclusivity fees" for personal interviews. Raphael had left a message that he was worried about me, but he didn't say anything about rescheduling our evening. And there were two messages from Paddy, the first saying he was at his parents' apartment, the second that he was going out for a while, but would call me at Sira's later. I wondered if there was a cop in my apartment listening in on all of this.

I dialed Paddy's folks in Brooklyn. His mother answered.

"This is Lydia, Paddy's friend."

"I know who you are," she said. From her tone, I knew Mrs. Riordin had been reading the afternoon papers.

"Is Paddy there?"

"No. He just banged in here, messed up my kitchen, and left."

"Messed up your kitchen?" I do all the cooking at our apartment for the simple reason that Paddy is culinarily impaired.

"That's right. Dumped everything on the counter and didn't put it back. Went through everything a dozen times and then gave up."

Now I got it. Paddy had been ice-pick hunting in his mom's kitchen. And apparently he had come up short. What the hell did that mean?

"Well, if you see him, tell him I called," I said.

Mrs. Riordin hung up without another word.

There was a pound of sliced corned beef in Sira's refrigerator; she had long ago given up trying to get her Jewish boy-friends to snack on paneer paratha and crispy murukkus. I peeled off a few slices and chewed them down in front of the open refrigerator. That was all the dinner I had the stomach for. Then I went over to the living area, picked up the package I had taken from Michael's room, kneeled down on Sira's rattan carpet, and unwrapped it.

It was the Lehmann first edition of Paul Bowles's *The Sheltering Sky,* the book that had awakened me with a start from my Brooklyn slumbers when I was sixteen. A bookplate pasted to the title page said, *For Lydia. This is just the beginning. Love, Michael.*

Sweet Michael's last gift for me. So thoughtful, so perfectly and painfully bittersweet.

I almost wept. I took a deep breath, opened the book at random, and began to read. In only minutes, I was alone in the Sahara—Kit Moresby, lost soul of all lost souls.

One never took the time to savour the details; one said: another day, but always with the hidden knowledge that each day was unique and final, that there never would be a return, another time. How many more times will you remember a certain afternoon of your childhood, some afternoon that's so deeply a part of your being that you can't even conceive of your life without it? Perhaps four or five times more. Perhaps not even. How many more times will you watch the full moon rise? Perhaps twenty. And yet it all seems limitless.

Reading Paul Bowles is the closest this lapsed Catholic ever gets to having a religious experience. I let the book slip out of my hands and closed my eyes.

It is hard to say precisely what I was feeling just then. Frightened, sure, but not nearly as frightened as I should have been given what Sira had so delicately referred to as my "situation." In fact, I found it disturbing that I wasn't more frightened of what might happen to me, which struck me as a sign that I was slipping into denial. Familiar territory, that. I certainly was also feeling abandoned. Sira's arm's-length note had rubbed salt in that particular wound, but it was Amy Liu's manipulations that had opened it wide. Yet, like the drone of a sitar, I felt an undercurrent of an altogether different emotion: I felt weirdly detached, the way people who have had near-death experiences are reported to feel when they peer into the abyss. I sat there for a long time.

I saw the envelope the moment I opened my eyes. It was jutting out from the last page of *The Sheltering Sky;* apparently it jarred free when I let the book drop. It was addressed to Michael at the Yale Club. The return address was *Deposito-Cassa der Stadt Bern.* Inside, on three separate sheets—one in French, one in German, and one in English—was the bank statement for Account #23509-55-33: 850,000 Euros.

How quaint—like many a patriotic American, Michael had kept a stash in a Swiss bank account, where it would be free from the prying eyes of the IRS. Had he left the statement inside the book by mistake? Or to impress me? I was stuffing the contents back into the envelope when I saw Michael's scrawl on the back of the French statement. It said, "L. Starter money for our new life. Memorize this number—it's ours. M." The word "ours" was underlined twice.

I felt my breath catch. Michael had actually been in possession of a thought-out, long-range *plan* involving me, Paris, kiosks, and oodles of money? It was not just those ephemeral, postcoital hormones drizzling on his brain? Not once had I really expected that. How touching, and how very sad. I never would have accepted. My heart suddenly beat in triple time: A secret, joint Swiss bank account for close to a million U.S. dollars is a flashing red neon sign of a murder motive! *Now what?* I could take the money and run. No personal obligations, nobody to share it with. And most significantly, with the account being in numbered code, no one even needed to know about its existence.

Unless, of course, somebody already did.

I took the envelope and statements into the kitchen, set them aflame with a stove burner, and watched them turn to ashes in the sink. I did not memorize the account number. Then I washed the sink and returned to the living room, where I stood on Sira's harp stool and slipped *The Sheltering Sky* behind the row of books on the topmost shelf of her bookcase. Okay, first I kissed the spine of the book, just as my mother kisses the spine of the New Testament every time she sets it down on her bed table.

Stepping back down, I saw an André Previn CD called *Sallie Chisum Remembers Billy the Kid*. I picked it up. Sallie Chisum is my favorite courtesan of the Wild West, a woman who bedded both Billy the Kid *and* Pat Garrett, the obsessed sheriff who ultimately shot Billy in the back. Ms. Chisum was an equal-opportunity courtesan. I didn't know her story had been set to music. I put "Sallie" on the CD player, stretched out on the floor beside Sira's harp, and slipped into a dreamless sleep.

The ringing telephone woke me. I looked at my watch: ten-fifteen. I'd slept for almost three hours. I picked up the phone, "Hello?"

"Lydia?" It was Paddy.

"It's good to hear your voice."

"Same here. How are you doing, pal?"

"Fine, I think. I was sleeping."

"I can call back later."

"No. I want to talk." I started to lean my back against the harp, but it rolled away from me. "I hear you mucked up your mother's kitchen."

"Still her bad boy after all these years."

"You were looking for her ice pick, weren't you?"

"Yes."

"And it wasn't there."

"No."

"I still think that's craziness," I said.

"Yup. So what have you been up to?" Paddy said.

I quickly ran him through my encounters with Sylvia, Danny Bloomster, and Amy Liu. I decided I'd tell him about my Yale Club interlude another time.

"No wonder you're exhausted," Paddy said when I'd finished.

I looked at my watch again: ten-thirty.

"Well, got to go," I said. "Or I'll be late."

"Lydia, you aren't actually going through with this thing with Bloomster, are you?"

"Yes," I said. Actually, I had just made that decision.

"Don't," Paddy said.

"You look for ice picks, I look for motives," I said.

"It could be dangerous, Lydia."

"I'm a big girl," I said.

"What's Bloomster's address?"

I told him.

"I'll be waiting for you at Sira's," Paddy said, and we said goodbye.

12

I sauntered into Morgan's Bar and Grille at ten after eleven. I had changed into a pair of jeans and a T-shirt from Sira's wardrobe. I figured Sira would not mind; also, I figured she owed me. The T-shirt had a picture of a harp on it, with the caption PLUCK YOU!

I took the stool next to his at the bar. This close, I could see patches of makeup at Bloomster's hairline and, behind his ears, remnants of the evening's performance. I wondered how many theater lovers actually came to The Loft Playhouse to see Bloomster reprise Pacino's role in *The Indian Wants the Bronx*. My guess was the theater was literally named—it was some buddy's SoHo loft—and it held twenty patrons, tops; but no matter what, only ten ever showed up. Undoubtedly, that was why Bloomster moonlighted as both surrogate and barkeep: He was also the theater's sole angel. But who was I to judge? I was in the philanthropy business myself.

"Want a drink?" Bloomster asked.

Actually, I didn't; I had started to feel fragile the moment I came upon Michael's Swiss bank statement, and alcohol would probably wreck me completely. But on the other hand, I definitely did not want to move the proceedings to Bloomster's apartment.

"I'll have some cranberry juice," I said.

"Nothing in it?"

"I don't want to dull my senses," I lied.

"Good girl," Bloomster said, closing a hand on my thigh.

I literally flinched. I shoved Bloomster's hand away with a force that surprised us both. He looked shocked. I felt giddy. The truth is, feeling repulsed by a man's touch made me feel—well, sort of virtuous. I don't think I'd responded this vehemently to a man's advances since my junior prom at St. Elizabeth's when a beefy-faced boy from Immaculate Conception High School cupped his hand over my crinoline-covered buttocks while we were waltzing to Johnny Mathis. I gave that boy a shove that made him trip backward into the gym wall. Among other things, whacking Bloomster made me feel vindicated—perhaps I was no different from Babycakes and her sisters in some fundamental way, but I was still discriminating: I do not accommodate assholes. I'd bet the ranch that Sallie Chisum had been discriminating too; yes, she'd opened her heart and her legs for both Billy the Kid and his assassin, but I'm sure she drew the line somewhere, probably at some soupy-eyed, low-rent, itinerant actor who thought he was God's gift to women.

The question, then, was what I thought I was doing sitting here with a wad of twenty-dollar bills making an obscene lump in my pocket? *Investigating, right? Undercover investigating.*

"Touchy, touchy," Bloomster was crooning beside me. "I take it you have some issues, darling."

Oh yes, I had some issues, all right. Like a barely controllable desire to dump my newly arrived glass of cranberry juice in his crotch.

"Let's get to know each other a bit," I said.

"Really? Don't we want to maintain the aura of mystery?"

"I'm not into mysteries." *Just one.*

"Well, let's start with your name then," Bloomster said.

"Everybody calls me Babycakes," I said, inspired.

Bloomster laughed. I took offense on behalf of Babycakes's memory.

"It's an old prep school nickname," I said.

"O-kay, Babycakes. So what do you want to know about me? Where I went to school? How long my dick is?"

No, dumping cranberry juice would be far too mild a gesture.

"Actually, I'm curious about your love life, Danny," I said.

"My *love* life?"

"Yes," I said as earnestly as I could. "With your work being what it is, is there still time for somebody special?"

Bloomster studied my face, suspicion in his high-wattage eyes. Instinctively, I reached into my pocket and withdrew five hundred dollars in twenties, fresh from a Madison Avenue ATM. "Let's get this part out of the way, okay?" I said as I handed it to him.

Bloomster stuffed the bills in his jeans and signaled the bartender for another Scotch. It is remarkable how much a money transaction changes the dynamic in a relationship. He offered me a smile and an expression that closely resembled gratitude, and I suddenly felt marvelously empowered. For a brief moment, I wondered if Frank and Abe and Raphael and Michael enjoyed that same feeling when they deposited their payments in my dresser drawer. I had not given that much thought before. I didn't feel like giving it much thought now, either.

"So?" I said. "*Is* there a certain somebody?"

"Who says they're separate?" Bloomster said.

"What's separate?"

"Work and love."

"You love one of your patients?"

Bloomster smiled. He patted the money in his pocket as if to make sure it was still there.

"It's Angelica, isn't it?" I said.

Bloomster kept smiling. "We have something special going," he said.

So Danny Boy and the Widow Linscott *were* a bona fide item! And unless Bloomster was a better actor than I believed him to be, his feelings for her were genuine. At least genuine enough to guiltlessly accommodate his career goals. Oh boy, I was getting my five hundred dollars' worth, but I needed to proceed with caution.

"Angelica feels the same about you," I said, sounding like a junior high school intermediary helping a shy couple arrange a rendezvous.

"I certainly hope so," Bloomster said.

"And now that Michael is, you know . . ." I let my voice drift off artfully.

Bloomster abruptly hopped off his stool. "Let's get going," he said.

"I'm happy here."

"I'm not," Bloomster said. He started for the door.

Ooops. Going to Bloomster's apartment was definitely not part of my plan, but there was way too much dangling to cut things short now. I followed him out onto the street.

"I imagine both you and Angelica will want to wait awhile before you—"

"I'm just around the corner," Bloomster said, not looking at me. He was walking so fast I had to break into a little trot to keep up with him. Maybe this was a bad idea, after all; maybe it was better to say goodbye to Bloomster right here and now. I could always tell Amy Liu, that manipulative little smarty pants, what I had learned, and let the homicide detective take it from there. She was the expert, after all.

We were now at the door to 185 Sullivan Street, and Bloomster was manfully inserting his key in the lock. He already had my money and he certainly had figured out that I was having second thoughts about tonight's "touch and response" tutorial. He could have very easily told me I shouldn't go through with it if I didn't want to—*and* kept my money in the bargain. I definitely doubted Danny Bloomster was being propelled by his work ethic. *So what, exactly, was on his mind?*

I had been in the reverse situation the night Abe Levanthal arrived for his first session. Abe hadn't wanted to go through with it. It was nothing personal, he told me, but the entire business made him feel dishonest and disloyal. He deeply loved his wife, Rose; she was the mother of his five wonderful children; she had stuck with him through bad times and good; she was a fine person, through and through, even if she had put on forty pounds in the past three years. Abe didn't know it, but I was as much a neophyte as he was that night. The *Learning to Love Again* video had not offered any tips about dealing with a patient's moral ambivalence. Abe had presented me with an envelope containing six one-hundred-dollar bills and started to put his camel's hair coat back on when I'd said, "For that much money, the least I can offer you is a drink."

"What do you have?"

"English port?"

"Okay, one glass," Abe had said, throwing his coat across my living room couch.

Over the next hour and a half, we drank the entire bottle and Abe talked. He talked about his poverty-stricken boyhood in the Bronx, his triumphs at the Bronx High School of Science, and then at Yale and Yale Law School. He talked about his wife and his children. And then he began to talk about growing older.

"It stinks," he'd said. "You've got eighty percent of your life behind you and pure shit in front of you. I call this part of life, 'Waiting for the diagnosis.' Every time I go to the doctor, I'm thinking, is this going to be it? Is this the time he's going to sit me down and say, 'Abe, I think it's time you got your affairs in order.'"

"I've had a terrific life," Abe had gone on, loosening his tie. "Better than I ever expected to have. So, no complaints there.

But memories are overrated. What's done is done, the past has passed. And when I wake up in the morning, I'm a sixty-six-year-old man who has had two heart attacks and who—"

Here, Abe had stopped, stood, and walked to my side window that catches half of the flood-lit Washington Square Arch. His back to me, he'd said, "A morning erection is a glorious thing, Miss Quess. It is an affirmation of life. Your beating heart made visible. And when it's gone, when you wake up each morning with nothing more than a wilted rosebud between your legs, you know your life is already over."

Abe had turned to look at me. There were tears in his dark eyes. And now mine started to water too. I have always had a weakness for poets.

"It is a peculiar idea, wanting to have desire," he'd said. "Wanting to want. Mourning a yearning. Peculiar as hell."

Then Abe started to cry in earnest, great sobs convulsing his body. I went to him and held him. He must have cried like that, full out, for a good ten minutes, and I could feel all that wracking sorrow beating against me and resonating inside me. And then, as his tears gradually subsided, I felt something else. Abe Levanthal had an erection and it was a good one. I tilted in against it. "Well, hello," I'd said. I wiped a tear from his eyes. "The Fountain of Youth."

"All I really want to do this time is talk," I said.

Danny Bloomster closed the door to his one-room apartment behind us. The interior looked nothing like I had imagined. It was all sharp angels and gleaming metal surfaces—more like an office in a hip Madison Avenue ad firm than a romantic bohemian boudoir.

"We'll play it by ear, okay, Babycakes?"

"Okay." I'd been playing it by ear all day.

"You seem very interested in Angelica and me," Bloomster said, sitting down on the edge of his bed. "Does that go back to prep school too? Some rivalry thing?"

So Danny Bloomster actually thought he was a therapist. Why should that surprise me? Sylvia Kahn thought she was one too. "We're a little competitive. Most friends are, aren't they?" I remained standing.

"About men?" Bloomster said. "Men and sex?"

"Maybe."

"Have you two ever slept with the same man before?" Bloomster's self-satisfied smirk was making a comeback.

"No," I lied again. Of course, Angelica and I had slept with the same man. *A man who was now dead.*

"So why now?" Bloomster asked. He was unlacing one of his sneakers, a simple act that made my skin crawl.

"I guess I want to get to know Angelica better," I said. "And getting to know you seems like a good way to do that. Don't you agree?"

Bloomster ignored the question. He unlaced his other sneaker, then kicked it off and stood up. "You really need to relax, Babycakes," he said finally.

"Are you thinking of marrying her now that you can?" I said.

Bloomster shrugged. It looked like an anxious shrug to me.

"Once the lawyers get everything straightened out, I mean."

"That's up to her, right?" he said.

"But that *is* the plan, isn't it?" I said.

"We haven't talked about it lately."

"Because you haven't been seeing that much of each other lately?" I ventured.

"It happens," Bloomster said. "Comes with the territory."

"Of bringing married couples back together with renewed passion?" I said, taking my words straight out of Sylvia's playbook.

"Whatever." With that, Bloomster padded in his socks to his bathroom.

So had Mrs. Linscott been busy transferring her erotic sensitivities *back to her husband*? It certainly *sounded* that way. Maybe that worked better for girls than it did for boys? I wouldn't have guessed it from Michael's behavior toward me. And though Angelica did not figure in Michael's future plans in Paris, she undoubtedly knew nothing about that. But where did that leave Danny Bloomster? For one thing, it left him without a wealthy angel for his dream theater.

To my left was a closet. I pulled open the door and peered inside. Danny Bloomster had a very impressive wardrobe, lots of Armani and Hugo Boss suits. One of these was a gray, pinstriped job. That in itself was unremarkable. But in the corner of the closet I also saw a little stack of boxes—wig boxes, if I was not mistaken. I was not. I opened the topmost box. Bingo, first try: It contained a finely crafted wig of close-cropped brown hair. An odd accessory for a man who himself possessed close-cropped brownish hair.

I shut the closet just as Bloomster returned, drying his

hands with a towel. I edged toward the apartment door, backing away slowly but talking fast. "Look, I'm thinking if you and Angelica have something special, then—"

Bloomster took two long steps across the room and grabbed me by the wrist.

"I really want to tell you everything," he said. "Everything you want to know, *Babycakes*. But this feels way too formal. I mean, it feels like a courtroom."

Interesting choice of metaphor. It was definitely time to go. I tried vainly to shake loose of his grip. Over Bloomster's shoulder, I could see his kitchenette. There was a knife rack over the stove, one knife missing. *What the hell was under the towel he was holding?*

"If you really want to talk—talk *openly*—then you've got to meet me halfway."

"What do you mean?" I asked. *I've got to get out of here!*

"I'm drawing a bath for you, Babycakes. A nice warm bath to get rid of all that tension. There's nothing like getting naked for stimulating candid conversation, is there?"

I was shaking. Bloomster grinned, tightened his grip on my wrist. He was obviously getting off on my panic. Was he completely nuts, a maniac—a *homicidal* maniac? Was he going to stab me and then call the police and tell them it was self-defense? Loud voices in the street below made us both glance toward the window for an instant.

"Just how stupid do you think I am?" Bloomster sneered, turning back to me.

"Wha . . . what are you talking about?" I stammered.

"You're wearing a wire!"

"You're crazy!"

"TAKE OFF YOUR SHIRT!"

"I'M GOING TO SCREAM!"

"What's new?" Bloomster laughed. Clearly, the tenants of 185 Sullivan Street were inured to the "sound effects" that regularly emanated from his apartment. "Take it off, Babycakes!"

Did he actually think I was wearing a wire? Is *that* what this was about?

"I can't take it off with you holding on to me," I said coolly.

Bloomster let go. My eyes darted to the door: The chain lock wasn't up, but surely the spring lock was engaged. I would have to spin around, release the lock, turn the knob, open the door, and run. Bloomster was only one step away from me and he had fast hands.

"Now!" Bloomster barked.

I crossed my arms in front of me, pulled the bottom of my T-shirt out of my pants, then started to lift it over my head. As usual, I was not wearing a bra.

"Nice tits," Bloomster said. "*Small,* but nice."

Pluck you! The T-shirt was in my hands above my head. I snapped it at Bloomster's face, catching him in the eyes. I spun around, unlatched the door, put my hand on the knob.

"You fucking bitch!" Bloomster screamed. He grabbed at me blindly. I turned the knob and pulled on the door.

"Lydia! Are you all right?" Paddy asked.

"Thank God!" I wailed. I crossed my arms over my chest and flung myself at him.

"Who the fuck is this?" Bloomster bellowed. What he saw was a florid-faced Irishman in a clerical dickey and a Yankees warm-up jacket coming through his door. Danny Bloomster may have been a Greenwich Village rake who thought he'd seen it all, but at this particular moment he was obviously in shock.

"Stay the fuck away from her!" Father Paddy Riordin shouted back at him, throwing his jacket over my shoulders.

I heard footsteps pounding up the stairway outside the door. Over Paddy's shoulder, I saw the guy who had answered the door earlier with a pair of NYPD patrolmen chugging up behind him. Perfect timing. "That's him!" the neighbor said, pointing at Paddy.

The cops stepped through the door, one grabbing Paddy's left arm, the other his right. Then the taller of the two pulled Paddy's hands behind his back and handcuffed him.

"Did he harm you, ma'am?" the other cop said to me, gesturing toward Paddy, but not looking me in the eye. The reason for that was he was looking at my breasts. I let him have a good look. I figure I was establishing some rapport with him.

"*That's* the one who attacked me!" I said, pointing at Bloomster and now clutching Paddy's jacket tightly around me.

"Bullshit!" Bloomster said. "She's crazy. Totally crazy and out of control."

"Definitely!" the neighbor chimed in. "They're in it together! She's been hunting Danny all day long. Came here looking for him this afternoon. And this clown—Bozo the Bishop—he shoved me against the wall so he could march right in here! I call that 'breaking and entering,' don't you?"

"May I please have my T-shirt?" I said. It was Sira's, after all.

The shorter of the cops retrieved my shirt from the floor and handed it to me, then attentively watched me wriggle into it.

"I have reason to believe that this man is a murderer," I said, gesturing toward Bloomster.

"She's totally nuts," Bloomster said. "I just met this woman. Picked her up in a bar a few minutes ago. Morgan's, around the corner. Ask anybody there. She was like a bitch in heat."

"Shut up, buddy!" my cop said. I could have hugged him.

"She pulls off her shirt and then, bang! She pulls a knife on me," Bloomster went on. "I screamed."

"We heard you, Danny," the neighbor said. "We heard you screaming downstairs, didn't we, guys?" He looked to the patrolmen for confirmation.

"I'm calling this in," the taller policeman said to his partner.

"I guess you'd better," the other cop said.

The tall one stepped into the hallway, removed his two-way radio from its holster, and turned his back to us. I could not make out most of what he said, but the words "domestic disturbance" jumped out a few times. He and the person on the other end of the call went back and forth a few times, apparently trying to figure out which protocol the situation demanded, when I saw him turn his head and stare intently at my face.

"Hold it a sec," he said into his radio. Then to me, "You were in the papers today, weren't you, miss?"

I nodded.

"I'm bringing them *all* in," he said into his radio.

13

I was permitted one phone call. Without a moment's hesitation, I dialed Amy Liu's cell phone and told her I was back at the Sixth Precinct, this time detained for disorderly conduct.

"You should have called a lawyer," Liu said. She sounded very tired and more than a little annoyed.

"I don't need a lawyer, I need help," I said.

"You need both, Lydia," she said. I found it heartening that at least she used my first name.

"I'm pretty sure I know who did it, Amy," I said.

"Did what?"

"Murdered Michael Linscott. I was just at his apartment and he tried to kill me too."

A long pause at the other end.

"And where is that party now?" Liu said.

"Here. Same charge, that is if you call trying to kill me disorderly conduct."

Another pause, although this time I could faintly hear a man's muffled voice somewhere near Amy's phone. This voice was saying, *"So, go! And while you're at it, go fuck yourself!"* Then Amy came back on and said she was on her way.

The cops had brought us to the station house in two separate police cars, Bloomster and his neighbor in the backseat of one, Paddy and me in the back of the other. The trip was only eight blocks, just enough time for Paddy to tell me how he happened to be standing outside Bloomster's door at that critical moment. He and Manuel had been distributing care packages when Paddy had what he called a "vision" of me being manhandled.

"A religious vision, I assume," I said. "Was I wearing my halo?"

"Right. The one with the dimestore glitter."

My cop, the breast aficionado, was driving, and I saw his baffled expression in the rearview mirror.

Paddy went on, saying that he had immediately driven his truck to the Sullivan Street address I'd given him and there engaged in a heated conversation with the man who answered the door—the angry neighbor. That was the shouting Bloomster and I had heard.

"I believe you saved my life, pal," I'd said to Paddy as we pulled up in front of the Sixth Precinct.

"Now all I have to work on is your soul," he replied.

Once inside, they separated Paddy and me. I do not know who he favored with his allotted phone call. I was fingerprinted for the second time in two days, then shut inside a small, fluorescent-lit room with a legal pad on which I was instructed to write my "statement." I was refining my fourth draft—my first began, "When in the course of human events"—when Captain Amy Liu knocked once, came inside, and sat down opposite me. She was in pressed Calvin Klein jeans and a sweatshirt with a University of Chicago logo. How the hell had she ended up in the homicide detection business? Just lucky, I guess.

"Okay, let's hear it," she said.

I gave her the long, nuanced version, beginning with my luncheon at the Plaza with Angelica Linscott, then my conversation with Sylvia Kahn, and finally my two encounters with Danny Bloomster. Once again, I omitted my adventure at the Yale Club; it did not seem propitious at this point for Captain Liu to know about that joint Swiss bank account. During my recitation I broke all promises—both explicit and implied—to both Angelica and Sylvia. Amy asked me to reiterate the events in Danny Bloomster's apartment in as much detail as I could.

"So at no point did he actually say he knew Michael Linscott had been murdered? Or even that he knew he was dead?" Amy said when I finished for the second time.

"Not in so many words, but—"

"Did he say if he had spoken with Mrs. Linscott since last night?"

"No. It sounded like he hadn't heard from her for a while."

"Did he actually say that he and Mrs. Linscott had been planning to get married or to live together or anything along those lines?"

"I told you what he said: 'We have something special go-ing.' That is pretty much along those lines, wouldn't you say?"

"Not necessarily," Amy said. "And exactly *why* do you think Mrs. Linscott had stopped seeing Mr. Bloomster and re-sumed a monogamous relationship with her husband?"

I went through all that again for her.

"Now this bath business," she went on. "Is that something that *you* have ever done with your own clients, Ms. Quess?"

"I like it better when you call me Lydia."

"No problem, Lydia. What's the answer?"

"Of course I have. I have a Jacuzzi. It's something lots of stressed-out people do before they make love. Even married couples."

"I wouldn't know."

"I thought you were married, Amy."

"I am. And I wouldn't know," she said. "So why did it strike you as so odd that he wanted you to get into the tub before you had sex?"

"For one thing, I had no intention of having sex with him and he knew that," I said indignantly. "I thought I'd made that clear to you."

"But I don't know how clear you made that to Mr. Bloom-ster," Amy said. "You gave him his five-hundred-dollar fee and you went back to his apartment with him. How clear could it be?"

"Jesus! What are you trying to lay on me? Haven't you ever heard of date rape, Captain Liu?" I was furious and my logic showed it.

"Tell me again what he said about suspecting that you were wearing an eavesdropping device," Amy said.

I told her again.

"That's a peculiar thing to be concerned about if you've got nothing to hide."

"Thank you," I said.

"And you've got to wonder what he meant when he said that he'd tell you everything you wanted to know once he was sure you were *not* wearing a wire."

"I don't think he meant anything by that except some kind of bluff," I said. "Why would he want to tell me anything— anything incriminating—even if I wasn't wired?"

"Maybe he was trying to get you to tell *him* something," Amy said. "Has either Bloomster or his neighbor ever been inside your apartment?"

"No. Not that I know."

"Okay, we've got their fingerprints and DNA now, so we'll check them against what we found at your place. I had a little talk with Bloomster before I came in here and he's agreed to let us check out his shoes too."

"He's got a whole closet full of them. And while you're there, check out that wig too."

"For what that's worth," Amy said. "I'm far from eliminating him, but to tell you the truth, Lydia, I don't think Danny Bloomster is our man."

"Why not?"

"Bloomster strikes me as a very frightened man. Frightened and extremely risk-averse. It comes with having a lot to hide."

"I don't follow."

"I believe Mr. Bloomster keeps more than wigs hidden in his closet," Amy said. "I got the impression that he and his neighbor are more than casual friends."

How come I didn't pick up on that?

"Well, say you're right—then maybe the two of them are behind this? For the money. The man I saw running out of my apartment looked *a lot* like Bloomster's pal and he was wearing pinstripes when I came by this afternoon. I'd get his shoe prints too."

"I've already arranged to do that," Amy said. "As I say, I'm not eliminating anybody yet."

"So Bloomster is *gay*? He's sure in a strange line of work."

"I don't know," Amy said. "Maybe it makes it easier for him in the long run. Just pure work, no complications. But I'm afraid I'm out of my depth when it comes to personal reasons for wanting to become a sex surrogate."

I took this as a personal insult.

"It's not that complicated, Amy," I said. "The money is good. Very good. Everybody makes compromises to keep their lives humming along. Some people are just clearer with themselves about what those compromises are, if you know what I mean."

From the expression in Amy's eyes, she took *this* as a personal insult. Which I'm pretty sure is what I meant it to be, although I couldn't say exactly what in Amy's life my target was. Possibly the man I overheard saying, *"And while you're at it, go fuck yourself!"*

Amy stood up. "As for you, Lydia, I think you are either guilty *or* you're crazy."

"I suppose I should be relieved it's not both."

"Actually, I doubt that you killed Linscott, although that's not my official opinion," Amy said, looking me steadily in the eyes. "But I do think you need to have a screw loose to go unprotected into the apartment of a man who you believe is a killer."

"Desperation has a way of making you do crazy things."

For what must have been a full minute, Amy Liu and I wordlessly eyed one another. Then she sat down across from me again and said, "The question is, just how desperate are you?"

"Very," I said. "I want to find out who killed Michael more than anybody. More than his widow, for sure. And probably more than you do."

Amy nodded. "Sergeant Wilson has already talked to both Abe Levanthal and Frank Macy. He's still trying to catch up with your Señor Raphael Llargos. Both Levanthal and Macy have solid alibis, but that means very little if this was a contract murder. And we have reason to believe that it was. Very professional job—quick, quiet, no prints on the weapon."

"So they're suspects too?" I said. "All three of them?"

"Of course."

"Why?"

"All three of them had an ongoing sexual relationship with you and so did the victim," Amy said. "That's graph number one in the big book of probabilities. The high-percentage suspects a colleague of mine calls 'lovers-in-law.'"

"These men are not exactly my lovers," I said.

"Maybe not to you."

"But it's not as if any of them don't know I have other clients."

"Knowing something and being at peace with it are two different things," Amy said.

Good point. Not all that original, but appropriate nonetheless.

"I'm sorry, Amy, but I find it very hard to believe that any of my clients could be jealous or possessive or crazy enough to kill anybody," I said.

"I'm sure you do," Amy said. "That's one of the charmless ironies of my line of work. If you know somebody—*really* know them—it's almost impossible to believe they are capable of murder. But nine times out of ten, there is only one degree of separation between the murderer and the victim. So if you knew the victim well, the murderer is usually somebody you know too."

I found myself captivated by the way Amy Liu explained things—even if she *was* sly as a fox. Or maybe because of it.

"You said the question was how desperate I was," I said.

"That's right." Amy Liu pushed a strand of black hair behind one ear and leaned across the table toward me. "Are you desperate enough to conduct your own interrogations of Levanthal, Macy, and Llargos? To try to get them to open up with you in the privacy of your bedroom?"

Whoa! At that particular moment, I could imagine any number of reasons why someone would suggest to Amy Liu that she go fuck herself. She was seductive as hell and she was always operating on her own agenda. But most infuriatingly, she consistently seemed to be one step ahead of me.

"I'll think about it," I said.

Once again, Amy stood, but once again, she hesitated a moment and sat back down.

"I'm going to take a chance with you, Lydia," she said. "I'm going to tell you something that's still highly classified."

"Okay." I reminded myself that Amy Liu was the most talented con artist I had ever met. "Go ahead."

"Your friend Frank Macy knew Michael Linscott. In fact, he had a personal grudge against him."

"Because of me?"

"Actually no," Amy said. I could see her gauge my reaction— was I disappointed by that? "They had a legal run-in. An acrimonious one. Macy lost and it cost him plenty. Both financially and professionally."

"How did you find that out?"

"A seven-minute Google," Amy said. "I plugged in the names of all your bedroom visitors in pairs. All possible combinations. Michael Linscott plus Frank Macy yielded twelve citations, most from *Forbes* and *Fortune*."

"Neither of them ever mentioned that to me."

"Why should they? Did either of them know you were seeing the other?"

"No," I said. "That's one of my rules."

"Macy was quoted in one of the articles as saying that he 'wasn't through with Michael Linscott.' Not exactly a death-threat, but in the realm."

"All that on Google?"

"Let me share a professional secret with you, Lydia. Google digs up more leads than the forensics lab, at a ratio of roughly ten to one. But Googling doesn't make for riveting drama on Court TV." Amy sat back. "By the way, if Macy did do it, he must have figured out your relationship to Linscott at some point. He certainly knew where to find him."

"So Frank did it," I managed to mumble. I was stupefied. *Frank?*

"I'm not sure of anything," Amy replied. "And I sure as hell can't *prove* anything."

"You want me to get him to talk?"

Amy nodded.

"How do we do that?" I felt immeasurably more clearheaded the moment I said "we."

"We wire up your apartment and you take it from there," Amy said. "I don't see any reason why we couldn't be up and running by tomorrow night."

"You'd wire it?"

"That's right. And we'll install a real-time monitor nearby in case any intervention is necessary."

"Like if somebody tries to stab *me* with an ice pick."

"For example." Amy paused a moment. "It probably wouldn't hurt to set up a surveillance camera either."

"Like a peep show."

"It's entirely up to you, Lydia," Amy said, leaning farther back from the table. "If it's not something you want to do, I'm certainly not going to try for a warrant."

I nodded. I considered my options. This tiny, windowless, fluorescent-lit room with its peeling piss-yellow paint was probably a fair approximation of what a cell up at Ossining

Penitentiary was like. In fact, it was probably a marked improvement on one.

"Exactly how do you get somebody to admit to you they committed murder?" I said.

"By making them trust you," Amy said in a heartbeat.

"The way you make me trust you," I said. "Almost, that is. Until I remember that you really don't give a shit about me."

Amy looked genuinely offended. "Like you say, everybody makes compromises to keep their lives humming along. I may be more aware of mine than you give me credit for."

I took that as a complicated gesture of friendship.

"But what's to keep some enterprising cop from selling these bedroom videos to HBO? Big-buck reality TV," I said.

"I'm very sorry about that photograph in the *Post*," Amy said. "Internal Affairs is looking into that now. It won't happen again."

"I suppose I could sue you people for that, couldn't I?"

"Possibly," Amy said.

"I'm not going to sue anybody," I said. "I just want my life back."

"I want you to get your life back too, Lydia," Amy said, and she stood. "And now I have to do some paperwork to get you out of here."

14

It was almost three in the morning when Amy Liu and I walked out of the police station. Paddy had been released two hours earlier, leaving a note with the desk sergeant that he was picking up his truck and would wait for me at Sira's. Amy said she would drive me there. I noticed that another can of Heineken and another Whopper wrapper had been added to her car's interior since I'd last been there. I gathered that Amy had ended up not having dinner with her family after all.

"I guess your husband is used to your unpredictable schedule," I said.

"And I'd guess that you've never been married."

"True. I have a commitment problem. Manhattan cliché, right?"

"Somehow I don't think I'd call your life a cliché," Amy said with the hint of a smile.

"Well, if I *was* married, I can't imagine my husband would approve of my schedule either."

"That would be the least of his objections," Amy said. "Of course, whatever a woman's job is, if she is dedicated to it, men consider *that* infidelity."

"Is your husband from the old school?"

"My husband barely went to school," Amy said.

Her cell phone rang and she answered it, listened for a minute, and then told her caller she would be right over.

"I'm afraid I'm going to have to let you off as soon as we find a cab," she said to me.

"What's up?"

Amy appeared to consider her reply, then said, "We may have a break in the Babycakes case."

"What kind?"

"It seems Babycakes had an extracurricular boyfriend. In addition to her pimp. A white boyfriend with short hair and a shorter temper. One of her girlfriends tipped us."

"They found him?"

"Yup. Picked him up and brought him in." Amy spotted a taxi idling in front of a doughnut shop a block away and she started for it.

"And you're going to interrogate him now?" I said.

"That's right. While he's still gathering his thoughts."

"I'd like to watch you do that, Amy."

"I'm afraid that's not possible," she said, pulling up behind the taxi.

"Make an exception."

"No can do."

"Please."

"Sorry."

"I might pick up some techniques for my undercover assignment," I said.

Amy turned in her seat and regarded me; I believe I saw a flicker of grudging admiration for my persistence in her eyes.

"Think of it this way," I said. "You'll be building up my trust in you."

Amy smiled. "Aren't you tired?"

"Yes. Aren't you?"

"Never," Amy said.

His name was Peter Bucsescu and he was being held at the Tenth Precinct on West Twentieth Street. A pair of undercover cops from "crime buster" detail—the floaters who look for violent crimes about to happen—had located Bucsescu at his favorite watering hole, The Blue Lagoon, on West Thirty-Eighth, just two blocks away from the murder scene.

Bucsescu had appeared neither shocked nor particularly upset when informed that Babycakes had shed her mortal coil, but he did have an alibi all ready to go. He'd been at the "Winner's Circle" Off-Track Betting parlor on Seventh Avenue all day long and he had a half-dozen names of fellow bettors to vouch for his presence there.

Amy produced a guest pass for me to wear around my neck, then led me to a narrow corridor with a floor-to-ceiling window that, she explained, was mirrored on the other side—the interrogation room. She introduced me as a "material witness" to the one other occupant of this corridor, a gray-haired woman in a broad-hipped pantsuit variation of the uniform Amy had worn earlier that day. Then Amy left. Fifteen minutes later, Bucsescu, manacled at both wrists and ankles, was ushered into the interrogation room by two cops, who sat him down on a metal chair behind a metal table. And then, through the multiplex-screen-size window, I saw Captain Amy Liu in her pressed jeans and snug sweatshirt, her shining black hair falling across one side of her oval face, come striding in. The lady had star power.

"Has he been read his rights?"

"Yes, ma'am."

"Take those off him," Amy said tersely to the two cops, gesturing at Bucsescu's chains.

The cops hesitated, as if to say Captain Liu didn't realize how dangerous this man was. It struck me as overacting, a little set piece in which Liu establishes herself as the prisoner's pal. *Make him trust you.* The cops removed the manacles and Liu dismissed them. The cops offered another over-the-top pantomime of hesitation, then walked out.

"So, Peter, how'd it go today?" Amy asked. "Make any big scores?"

"What are ya talkin' about?"

"The ponies. Pick any winners?"

"Win some, lose some."

"How about the trifecta at Belmont?"

"Didn't play it."

"Really? Why not?"

"I'm a cautious bettor."

"That's not what I hear."

"From who?"

"Friends of yours."

Amy hadn't mentioned anything to me about Bucsescu's buddies. When had she found time to talk to them?

"They're full of shit," Bucsescu said. I noticed he didn't try to meet Amy's eyes; I think they made him uneasy. His own eyes looked glazed and low wattage.

"How long have you been going with Babycakes?" Amy Liu said.

"I wasn't *goin'* with Babycakes, I was *fuckin'* her. She's a whore, right?" Bucsescu let loose a truly repulsive smile that instantly reminded me of Danny Bloomster's.

"I see," Amy said. "So you were a john like all the rest."

"Not exactly."

Amy rested one Calvin Klein–clad buttock on the metal table directly in front of the interogatee. It was an incredibly provocative move.

"No, I didn't figure you for a paying customer," she said with a knowing smile.

"Why pay when she was givin' it away free, right?"

"Exactly." Amy kept smiling. "What time was the Belmont trifecta today?" she said.

Man, she kept the conversation bouncing off the walls.

"I dunno. Three, three-thirty. The usual."

"But you didn't bet on it."

"I tol' you already."

"You were otherwise engaged."

"I didn't have a tip. No tip, no bet."

"So you thought you'd knock off a piece of ass just to pass the time until the next race started," Amy said. The woman was a wordsmith.

"I didn't say that."

"Why would she give it away free to you, Peter?"

"Maybe she liked me."

"I bet she did," Amy said. "I bet you gave her something she didn't get from anybody else."

"I don't usually get any complaints," Bucsescu said, flashing that smarmy smile again.

Amy glanced at his crotch as if she might just ask him to show her the impressive goods. She was shameless.

"Actually, I hear Babycakes was giving it away free to a lot of dudes," she said.

"Bullshit!"

"Can't really blame her," Amy went on as she shifted her weight to her other buttock, stretching her jeans across her pubic area in the process. "I mean, that black stallion? You know, the one they call 'Raw Meat.' Hell, Babycakes was willing to pay *him* for some of that action."

"You don't know what the fuck you're talking about," Buscescu snarled.

"Didn't Babycakes tell you about him?"

"Shut the fuck up!"

"I say the bitch deserved it. Don't you, Petey?" Amy said.

"You fuckin' chink! You don't know shit!"

Buscescu's face had gone red, his eyes hardened. Suddenly,

he began to rise from his chair. Next to me, the gray-haired lady cop reached for a phone on the side wall. "We've got him covered!" she growled into the speaker and I heard her words echo inside the interrogation room. Bucsescu sat back down.

Amy very leisurely stepped away from the table toward the door, then stopped and, without facing Bucsescu, said, "You're wasting my time. The desk clerk saw you come into the hotel with Babycakes at three o'clock. Heard you punish her, saw you slip out with blood on your shirt. He'll ID you in the lineup easy. So I don't need shit from you, little man." She paused, then swung around to face him. "Unless you want to do yourself a favor and see if you can avoid doing life. Or worse."

Bucsescu looked terrified. "He was *sleeping*. He didn't see *shit*," he said.

"You saw *him, he* saw you. But what he doesn't know is how Babycakes provoked you. Pushed your buttons. It's called 'mitigating circumstances,' Petey. The kind judges take into account when they pass out sentences."

I watched Peter Bucsescu listen to her and go through what was obviously a laborious process for him: thinking. "What are you saying, lady?"

"I'm saying only you can tell us exactly what happened in there. How Babycakes gave you no choice."

"Fuckin' right," Bucsescu replied.

Amy opened a drawer on the table, withdrew a legal pad and pen, and set them in front of Bucsescu.

"Write it down, all of it," she said. "Tell it just like it happened. How she was just asking for it, you know? How she *made* you do it."

Bucsescu stared at Amy for a couple of seconds and then, *unbelievably,* he picked up the pen and began to write.

A few minutes later, Amy returned to the viewing corridor with Bucsescu's two-page confession, signed and witnessed, in hand.

"Surgical," the gray-haired cop said to her, smiling. "Under ten minutes. Nice."

"I could have paced it slower, I suppose," Amy said. "But I was getting hungry."

"No sense in wasting your 'A' material on a moron," Grayhair said.

"But *I* missed the nuances," Amy laughed.

The other woman laughed too. Clearly, the two of them were discussing an art form.

Back in Amy's car, I peppered her with questions. Where and when had she gotten all that background material, like the exact time of the trifecta ("I checked it on the Web") and the man's friend who said he was an incautious bettor ("Anybody who plays the horses is impulsive by definition. And everybody's got a friend who'll say some kind of shit about him behind his back").

"So you made that part up?" I said.

"I made most of it up."

"The hotel clerk didn't identify Bucsescu?"

"Are you kidding?"

"How about the fact that Babycakes was giving it away free to other men?"

"A no-brainer," Amy said. "Bucsescu *thought* that was what

she was doing. He's the jealous type. Hair-trigger. Textbook. All that macho swagger is a dead giveaway. Did you see his eyes? The man has serious self-doubts."

"That doesn't exactly make him unique," I said, a tad defensively. Amy was taking over my area of expertise, male sexual self-esteem.

"Tell me about it," Amy said.

"But what's-his-name? 'Raw Meat'? The black stallion?"

Amy grinned. "Inspired, wasn't it?"

"You made him up too?"

"Of course."

"You're kidding me."

"Babycakes was killed in a frenzy in a bedroom," Amy said. "Bucsescu might as well have had 'sexual rage' etched on his forehead. And I don't think there's a white guy in America who doesn't have nightmares about black men with monster dicks."

"But that name—'Raw Meat'?"

"Sometimes I think I should have been a poet," Amy said.

The morning sun had just begun to streak across the side streets leading in from the East River when Amy stopped in front of Sira's apartment building.

"So you beat the percentages on that one, didn't you?" I said.

"We got lucky with the girlfriend's tip. You can't factor luck into the probabilities," Amy said. She looked at me. "So, Lydia, did you learn anything useful tonight?"

"Yes, the hips," I said, smiling. "It's all done with the hips."

15

There was a second note taped to the scroll of Sira's harp, this one from Paddy:

> L,
>
> *I waited and worried. Called downtown and they said you'd left with Captain Liu, so I figured you were okay. Tried to sleep, but got the willies. It's the harp. From the couch, it looks like it's creeping up on you—maybe Heaven isn't so tranquil after all. Anyway, I borrowed a blanket and now am going to Grand Central to bed down with my cronies.*
>
> > *Hell may be more restful.*
> >
> > *Take care of yourself, pal. See you tomorrow back home.*
>
> *Love, P.*

The harp did not bother *me* in the least. I slept like an angel until after three in the afternoon.

Three of the ten new messages on my answering machine were from Frank. (Only one was from the media this time—the *Wall Street Journal*. They had probably done a little internal Googling.) Frank wanted to see me badly and as soon as possible. In his second and third messages, he added that he was terribly worried about me. I now had reason to believe Frank's most pressing worries were closer to home; in any event, his calls simplified matters.

I reached him on his cell phone. From the chatter in the background, I gathered he was in the trading room, although at ten to four, I knew the Stock Exchange was about to close. "I've been worried about you," he said yet again.

"I'm doing fine, Frank," I said. "But I'm glad you called. I'd like to get together too."

"Greatness," Frank said. It was an expression he had picked up from a Saudi classmate when we were all at Harvard Business School.

"How about tonight?"

"More greatness," Frank said.

"Six o'clock then?"

"Perfect. What room are you in?"

"Room? Oh, I'll be back home. I'm on my way there now."

A long pause at his end.

"I'd rather we met at the hotel," Frank said finally. "The Sherry."

I never told him I was at the Sherry-Netherland. He must have been reading the *Post*.

"I checked out. All's clear and I can reclaim my bedroom again," I said.

"What do you mean, 'All's clear'?"

"The police are done doing whatever they had to do," I said.

"So, does that mean they've solved it?" Frank was trying much too hard to make the question sound casual.

"Not even close," I said, then immediately wondered if that was the right thing to say. One ten-minute, on-the-job training session with Amy Liu was not going to carry me very far in the interrogation business.

"That's . . . that's unfortunate," Frank said.

"They're really stuck," I said. "Whoever did this is incredibly clever."

"So they don't think it's you," Frank said.

"Why should they, Frank?" If I had been harboring even an ounce of guilt about trying to manipulate Frank into spilling his guts, that was now gone.

"I don't know," Frank said. "I just figured—"

"Don't believe everything you read in the newspapers," I said.

"Listen, I'll pay for a hotel room. I just wouldn't feel comfortable at your place. Not yet."

"Haunted house?"

"Something like that."

This was not going according to plan. My bedroom was being wired, not some hotel room. To do that, Amy probably *would* need a warrant.

"Don't be silly, Frank," I said.

"If we're going to talk, I need to feel—you know—at ease."

"*Talk,* Frank?" I was trying to sound sexy, a verbal shifting of the buttocks on a table.

"Amongst other things," Frank said.

I had no choice. "The Sherry, then," I said. "At six."

I immediately called Amy on her cell and told her about the change in venue.

"Fuck," she said.

"It may come to that," I said.

"Your apartment is ready to go, so now this becomes an economic problem," she said.

"How so?"

"The budget for your case is already overextended. It'll be a real stretch to get the department to spring for a room at the Netherland. And I know for a fact that all the surveillance trucks are booked." Amy paused a moment. "Not to mention my personal life."

"Mention it."

"We've got a sitter for tonight. A rare occasion. And I've got a gallon of baby oil that needs to be rubbed on the man of the house. Ego problems. He's been feeling neglected."

"I'm sorry," I said.

"For who?"

"Both of you." I meant it. I had an inspiration. "Tell you what, Amy, I'll pay for the room. You do the monitoring, then keep the room for the night and have an intimate party with your hubby. Frank will be gone by eight at the latest, so that will give you lots of time. I'll even throw in room service."

Amy laughed. "That would be absolutely wonderful if it didn't break about a thousand rules, several of which would immediately relieve me of my rank and probably my job too."

"Okay, but look, I don't need a chaperone," I said. "Can't you just give me a little tape recorder to hide? Frank's not going to hurt me."

"We can't take that chance," Amy said. "I'll call you back, okay?"

"Okay."

I treated myself to another few slices of Sira's corned beef while I waited.

"Guess what? I got them to spring for the hotel room," Amy said when she called back. "I think it's my bonus for cracking the Babycakes case. They're getting some terrific PR out of that already—it proves that we *do* care about the little people after all."

"I appreciated that part too," I said.

"I'll meet you in the lobby of the Sherry-Netherland in an hour," she said.

"What about your personal life?"

"I don't know—maybe it *is* time I broke a rule or two," Amy said.

I left Sira a note thanking her for her hospitality and telling her I owed her for corned beef, but that was all I felt like saying. There is nothing like being a murder suspect to focus the mind on one's relationships. Sira's and mine definitely needed some reassessing.

I had the cab wait for me in front of Saks while I picked up the clothes I had left there, then had the cabbie drop me off at the Sherry-Netherland. Frank had already reserved a room for us, so all I had to do was pick up the key. Less than five minutes later, Captain Amy Liu came in through the front door in a tan linen pant suit, looking like a million dollars. Two steps behind her, carrying an Adidas gym bag, was a stocky, baby-faced man with Irish coloring and thinning hair. He was wearing a shiny blue suit and looked like fifty dollars in small bills. *Mister* Amy Liu. Yes, indeed, Amy was taking her full bonus. Good for her.

Amy made a quick business of introducing us ("Lydia, my husband, Barry; Barry, Lydia"), registered, then all three of us rode up in the elevator to the tenth floor without speaking a word. Barry went off to their room, 1043, while Amy accompanied me to mine, 1049. There, she planted three radio mikes: one in the lamp on the telephone table next to the bed, one in the drapes, and one on top of the medicine cabinet in the bathroom.

"Don't put on the radio or the TV if you can help it," she said as she started to leave.

"No problem. Any last-minute instructions?"

"Yes—be patient, tread lightly, and scream if you need help." Amy put a hand on my shoulder. "Any last-minute instructions for me?"

"Yes," I said. "Make him realize how lucky he is."

Amy smiled. "Nobody needs to know about Barry's being here, right?" she said.

"Of course not."

After Amy left, I showered and changed into my beige cot-

ton slacks and chocolate-brown cashmere sweater. Then I sat
in the Regency chair by the window and waited for Frank Macy.

**Frank and I started sleeping together on his honey-
moon.**

At least that is the way he likes to put it. He had gotten
married to his college sweetheart, Cindy, the week before classes
started our first term at Harvard Business School. We had met
in the registration line that first day, discovered we were in all
the same classes, and joined the same study group. I liked
Frank from the start; he was lean and funny and irrationally
worried about dying young. He failed to mention that he was
married until after we'd slept together in my dorm room several times, and when he did confess it, he declared that he
would get divorced immediately and marry me.

I, of course, had laughed. I was disappointed by his decep-
tion, sure, but mostly I was relieved. I had recently ended an
affair with my philosophy professor at Barnard, a man who had
taught me a great deal, none of it about sex. So I wasn't looking for commitment, I was looking for recreation. Frank was
a vigorous and enthusiastic lover, all I could ask for at the
time. My philosophy professor had had some "touch and response" problems. So I told Frank that what he did with Cindy
was entirely up to him, but as far as I was concerned, he could
have his cake and eat it too. And that's the way it's been with
us—off and on—for almost nine years. Frank and Cindy bought
a house in Montclair, had two children, and prospered. I had

two very brief and pointless affairs, made a name for myself in the corporate world, did irreparable damage to that name, and went into another line of work. Throughout, Frank stuck in there.

When I first told Frank about my arrangement with Sylvia's patients, he reacted the same way he had in my dorm room years earlier: He proposed to me. I reacted to *that* the same way I had years earlier. I explained that we had already agreed I was a kept woman, and that neither of us had a problem with that. Now I was simply expanding my career.

"I guess I'm just a hypocrite," Frank had said.

In the last few years, I have heard every man I slept with utter that very same line at one time or another. Often, I think that the chief effect of the liberation movement on the male masses has been their mastery of this line—"I guess I'm just a hypocrite." It liberates *them*.

"What you and I have is unique," I'd reassured Frank. And I'd meant it, even though I suspect that what *any* two people have is unique in some meaningful sense. But this may have been easier for me to understand than it was for Frank.

The only time the subject ever came up again was when Frank and I had scheduling discussions. If I said that a particular time to meet was not good for me, he would get sullen, but he always seemed to get over it quickly.

"I guess I'm a hypocrite," Frank said after he kissed me hello. I kid you not, those were his exact words.

"Really? What kind of hypocrite?"

"Garden variety," Frank said. "This whole business has got me incredibly nervous. You know, about me and Cindy. And me and my career."

But not worried about me.

"And about you too, of course," Frank added quickly.

Of course.

"What have you got to be nervous about, Frank?" I said.

Was I going too fast? Not treading lightly enough?

"I've kept this part of my life separate for so long, it would be a shame to have it come out now. And in this awful way," Frank said earnestly.

What I needed were some props—something to fuss with while we chatted. For misdirection.

"Are you hungry?" I said.

"Huh? No."

"I'm famished. Let's order up, okay?"

"Sure, whatever," Frank said, irritation in his voice.

Maybe I was bouncing too fast—cutting him off like that. In any event, I dialed down to room service and ordered eggs Benedict and a bottle of champagne. For a split second, I considered having a second bottle of champagne delivered to Amy and Barry's room to add to their festivities, but I thought better of it.

"Have the police talked to you?" I said.

"Yes. Only at my office, thank God. I got some suspicious looks there. He came in uniform."

I pictured Sergeant John Wilson, all three hundred pounds of him, being ushered into Frank's office at Salomon Smith Barney.

"I trust you told your colleagues it was just a parking infraction," I said.

"No, I said it was none of their business."

Not very smart, Frank. Could he really be the mastermind behind a perfectly executed contract murder?

"I don't think you have to worry about Cindy finding out anything from the police," I said. "They've been extremely discreet so far."

"It's not the police I'm worried about, Lydia. It's the newspapers."

"That *was* an unfortunate photograph, wasn't it?" I said.

"You certainly did look frivolous for the morning after a murder."

"I meant the *other* photograph, Frank. The one with the ice pick."

"Not a very flattering shot of Michael either," Frank said without a trace of irony.

That was one weird thing to say. Or was it? If it was a joke, it was hardly appropriate. And referring to Michael by his first name—that struck me foolhardy under the circumstances. I checked our positions: Frank appeared to be speaking in the direction of the drapes. Good.

"I haven't been granting any interviews with reporters, if that's what you're worried about," I said.

"I am very glad to hear that. It's probably better for both of us."

"And Sylvia—Dr. Kahn—doesn't even know your name. Although I don't think she will be talking to the newspapers either." Actually, I was not entirely confident that Sylvia

wouldn't blab to the press; Angelica's observation that psychologists are incurable narcissists had a compelling ring to it.

"I knew you never should have gone into this . . . this
thing," Frank said.

"You mean the fucking-for-dollars thing?" I said. I was trying to catch the rhythm and texture of Amy's interview with
Bucsescu.

"I wish you wouldn't talk that way," Frank said. He sounded
positively puritanical.

"Where did you and Michael meet, by the way? In my
lobby?"

"What?" Frank loosened his Princeton tie, sat on the edge
of the bed. Next to the lamp microphone.

"Michael told me the two of you knew one another. He
never told me how you met," I said, making it up as I went
along.

At that moment, there was a sharp rap on the hotel room
door. *Amy already? Did she detect some perilous threat I hadn't
picked up on? Was she going to bellow, "We've got him covered!"
through the door?*

"Room service."

"Lovely. I'm starving."

I opened the door and a room steward wheeled in a brass
trolley holding a magnum of Mumm in an ice bucket and a
covered dish. My Sherry-Netherland interrogation of Frank
was easily going to cost him a couple thousand. Fine with me.
"Win some, lose some," as Peter Bucsescu said minutes before
he lost some.

"Should I decant it for you?" the steward asked.

"Yeah, but I'd take the cork out first," I quipped.

Distraught as he was, Frank had to smile at that. My crack made the steward nervous and the cork got away from him as he popped it from the bottle. It shot, bullet-like, at the drapes. *What the hell did that sound like in Room 1043? A shot between the eyes?* "Boy! I have never seen a CORK shoot out like that before, have you, Frank?" I said, directing my voice at the drape mike.

The steward left, and Frank handed me a champagne flute, then clinked his against mine. "To better days," he said. We drank.

"As you were saying," I said, sitting down in front of the trolley and lifting the cover off my eggs. The Sherry-Netherland's eggs Benedict looked remarkably like Egg McMuffins. Who knows, maybe they got them from the same supplier? No matter, that four-star chef interviewed in the *New Yorker* swore Egg McMuffins were a gourmet treat.

"I wasn't saying anything," Frank said.

"About you and Michael," I prompted, taking my first bite. Definitely *not* McDonald's. More's the pity.

"We knew each other casually," Frank said. He emptied his glass, refilled it.

"From work?" I said, taking a second bite. Having a fork as a prop *did* help. No wonder they were always sitting down to dinner in those talky British *Masterpiece Theater* plays.

"Sort of," Frank said.

This was going better than I would have ever guessed it would. I figured it was time for another Amy Liu wall bounce. "Does Cindy read the *Post*?" I asked.

"No. She only listens to 'All Things Considered.'"

"You really are a lucky man, Frank," I said. I held my glass out for a refill. "Oh, I know. You know each other from that First Boston business. With Smith Barney."

I did not have the vaguest idea what I was talking about. But apparently Frank did. He set his glass down on the trolley. I believe he did that to avoid spilling champagne on his J. Press blazer—his hand was actually trembling. Oh yes, indeed, I *had* learned a thing or two at the Tenth Precinct last night: *Ask questions like you have attention deficit disorder, then shoot from the hip.*

"I have never seen a grown man lie with a straight face like that before in my life," he said caustically. He refilled his glass for a second time.

"And it was such a refined face too," I said.

"That's how those WASP fuckers do it," Frank said.

As far as I knew, Frank was a WASP himself, although judging by the irregularity of his features, his people had probably crossed the Atlantic a century or two later than the Linscotts.

I set down my fork, stood, and walked slowly toward him, giving my finely tailored slacks a little tug across my hips. Then I sat down on the bed and touched the side of his face with my fingertips.

"I promise you, I will do absolutely everything in my power to keep Cindy or anyone else from knowing about us. Just like I always have," I said softly, aiming my voice over Frank's shoulder toward the table lamp.

At that moment I fully understood that Amy Liu's line of

work was far more duplicitous and basically unethical than my own. That may have been the reason I found it so interesting.

"Thank you, darling," Frank said. "I knew I could count on you. I just needed to be reassured."

I kissed him on the neck, then whispered, "I would never have accepted Michael as a client if I'd had any idea of the history between you two."

"Is that true?" Frank said. He looked pleased. He reached for the Mumm and poured us each another glassful.

"Absolutely," I said. "I try to keep things separate in my life, just like you do. And that definitely crosses the line for me."

"It really does, doesn't it?"

"It must have been awful for you when you figured out that he was one of Sylvia's referrals," I said. "Like some kind of bad karma or something."

Frank smiled. "It's funny, but my first reaction was just the opposite. I thought, 'So the lying bastard can't even get it up. Serves him right.'"

"Really?"

Frank took a long, fifty-dollar sip of champagne. "Actually, I hated it, Lydia," he said, looking at his glass. "I mean, first he beats the shit out of me in court on that proxy business, and now he's sleeping with the love of my life."

"I wish you had said something. You know . . . before it came to this."

I waited for Frank to react to this last, casually dropped bombshell. When he said nothing, I asked, "How did you find out, by the way?"

"Find out what?"

"You know, that Michael was a client of mine."

Frank shrugged. "By accident. I'd had dinner in your neighborhood and I was walking by on the other side of the street when I saw Linscott come out of your building."

"It's a big building. He could have been visiting anybody."

"Like you said, it felt like bad karma the moment I saw him strutting out of there with that cocky expression of his. Like the guy was haunting me. Flaunting it in my face. So I crossed the street and I asked what's-his-face at the door who he had been visiting."

"Agron?"

"Right, Agron. He told me Michael had been in your apartment."

Giving out that kind of information was not exactly part of a doorman's job description.

"I'm so sorry, Frank," I said. I took one of his hands in both of mine before continuing. "Don't ever say this to anyone, but if anybody had to die—you know, of the men I see—I am glad it was Michael. He was not a nice man. Not at all."

Frank looked me full in the face. "He abused you?"

I bit down on my lower lip, nodding slowly. I don't think I was any worse an actor than, say, Danny Bloomster. In any event, my performance was good enough to get the desired effect: Frank was livid.

"The fuckhead!" he cried. "I'll tell you the truth, Lydia— I'm glad he's dead!"

So there it was, loud and clear enough to be picked up in stereo in Room 1043.

Only one step away from a full confession.

It *was* a crime of passion, after all, just as Amy's book of probabilities predicted it would be. Sure, that court case started it all, but it certainly sounded like Frank's relationship with me was what had put it over the top and into the realm of homicide. The murderer *was* a "lover-in-law," a paramour who felt betrayed and humiliated. In some way, I found it moving that Frank's feelings for me were so intense they could lead him to murder. But mostly what I felt was guilt. I was partially responsible for Michael's death. Being a self-styled, twenty-first-century courtesan wasn't as innocent and romantic as I had convinced myself it was.

But there would be plenty of time to think about all that. Right now, I needed to tie this up. Time for closure. Time to nail Frank. I pulled his head to my cashmere-sheathed bosom and said, "Sometimes, you just have to take things into your own hands, don't you, Frank?"

"Yes. Oh, yes," Frank whispered into my chest.

"YES. OH, YES," I echoed, verbatim. Did that make it hearsay evidence?

"You will never tell anyone, will you?" Frank said.

"No, never," I said.

"Neither will I, Lydia," Frank said. "I love you too much to tell anyone."

It was ending—and not with a bang, but a whimper. I felt so sad for both men, right then.

Frank pulled his head back. "You can always say it was self-defense," he said.

"Excuse me?"

"If it comes to that," Frank said, looking me steadily in the eyes. "If they are finally able to tie the murder to you."

"To *me?*"

"Yes. You can say Michael was about to hit you again and you just couldn't take it. That you had no choice, really."

"I don't know what you are talking about, Frank."

"Darling, I meant it—I won't tell a soul. Promise. Your secret is safe with me."

"Stop it, Frank!"

"Stop what?"

"It's just you and me. You can stop the bullshit."

"I don't know what you are talking about, Lydia."

"Don't you?" I shouted. I knew that was a bad move the moment I heard the shrillness in my voice. Amy had never sounded shrill with Bucsescu. Hell, she had barely raised her voice. Time to reign in. Time to regroup. I rested my head on Frank's shoulder. "I'm sorry. I'm a little overwrought these days."

"I can understand that," Frank said, stroking my hair.

"Really. I promise not to tell a soul," I whispered.

"Good."

"It's just between you and—I don't know, Frank—your conscience, I guess."

Frank abruptly stood up, thumping the side of my head with his shoulder in the process. "Good God, Lydia, you don't actually think *I* murdered him, do you?"

"I could hardly blame you, darling," I said. It was a slight variation on Amy's line, *"I say the bitch deserved it. Don't you?"*

"Lydia! For Christ's sake, how could you think such a thing?"

"It must be awful to have to keep a secret like that, Frank. No one to share it with. I just don't want you to feel alone."

"You're not serious, are you?" He truly did sound incredulous.

"I'm seriously concerned about you, if that's what you mean," I said.

"I didn't murder anybody!" Frank bellowed. His face turned an unattractive purple.

"I think you did, dear," I replied pleasantly.

"Fuck you, Lydia!"

"No, fuck *you*, Frank!" I'd had enough. "Get the hell out of my sight!"

Frank slowly tightened his tie and then, very deliberately, took another long swig of champagne. Textbook male behavior: Frank was demonstrating that yes, he would leave, but he would take his own sweet time about it. Several silent minutes later, he let himself out. I hoped the Sherry-Netherland cashier really socked it to him.

I poured myself another glass of Mumm and sipped it by the window. I could see clear across Central Park to the new Trump skyscraper at Columbus Circle. I read somewhere that some people believe ugly buildings cause cancer—their hideousness compromises the immune system. Maybe Donald Trump will end up shelling out in a class-action suit just like the tobacco companies did. I could not make head nor tail out of what had just gone on with Frank. Was he actually innocent and had only arranged to see me so he could ask my help in keeping his wife from finding out about our relationship?

Or was Frank smarter—and more cunning—than I gave him credit for?

Maybe he had guessed I would be wired and this was his opportunity to make a seemingly innocent claim of innocence?

The magnum of champagne was still more than half full. I wanted to finish it, but not alone. I lifted it, ice bucket and all, and walked out the door and down the hallway to Room 1043. I was about to knock on Amy's door when I heard her voice inside. Well, not exactly her voice—her *moans*. And punctuating these moans, like a bassoon obbligato, were grunts, courtesy of her husband, Barry. The sounds of sex.

I placed the ice bucket on the carpet just outside their door and shook my head.

Any woman listening carefully would know that Amy Liu was faking it.

16

I walked down Fifth Avenue until I reached Forty-Second Street, then hailed a cab across from the library. I was anxious to get home, even though I'd have to sleep in the living room until I got a new bed. The cabbie let me off directly in front of my building.

I never made it to the door.

Two steps away from the curb and an arm closed tightly around my waist. I was about to scream when a hand clapped over my mouth. Then I was yanked into the rear of a limousine. The car door slammed shut and the limo sped off, its tires screeching. We were a block away before I could finally twist around and see the face of my abductor.

It was Raphael. My Wednesday-nighter.

Just over two years ago Sylvia phoned to tell me she had a new patient for me, but before I signed on, I would need some special training. The man in question, a Señor Raphael Llargos, was an independently wealthy *bon vivant* from Argentina and he was willing to pay way above scale—fifteen hundred per session, to be exact. I informed Sylvia that I was available for special training. I met her at her office that evening.

"It is a case of poor sexual self-esteem," Sylvia began.

"Isn't it always?" I said. "I think you should call your first book *The Little Sexual Self-Esteem Engine That Could.*"

"This is different," Sylvie said. "Señor Llargos is so self-conscious he has been unable to have sexual relations with *anyone.*"

"My first virgin," I said. "What's wrong with him—is he incredibly ugly?"

"On the contrary. He's *exceptionally* good-looking."

"Let me get this straight, Sylvie—he's rich *and* he's good-looking, but he's got a formidable sexual self-esteem problem. What's wrong with this picture?"

"It's a physical problem." Sylvia leaned forward across her desk. "His organ."

"Yes?"

"Small, Lydia. Very."

"That's not a problem for me." God knows, Abe Levanthal was not particularly well endowed, but he made up in agility what he lacked in dimension; the man knew how to play the angles.

"Two inches," Sylvia said. "Erect."

I laughed. "Come off it."

"Get it all out of your system now, Lydia," Sylvia said sternly.

"But if you so much as smile when he drops his pants, I think he might kill himself. Seriously."

I stopped laughing. "I didn't know they came that small," I said.

"It's a genetic anomaly."

"But they have operations for that, don't they? I saw something on the Discovery Channel about how half the penis is trapped inside the body, just waiting to be set free by a nice surgeon. So, two times two is four. That's in the ballpark, isn't it?"

"Not possible. Llargos is a bleeder. Blood disorder, also genetic. Can't even have a tooth pulled. He's stuck with what he's got."

"Poor guy," I said. "What do I do? Just ignore it?"

"No, he's entirely too smart and self-conscious for that," Sylvia said. "You have to acknowledge it, but convince him that he still turns you on. That you are eager to have sex with him."

"I'm not sure I can do that," I said truthfully.

One of the secrets of my success in the surrogate biz is that I never have to resort to theatrics. Although I never would have predicted it, I actually *am* turned on by my clients—every one of them, so far. Arousing a man who has been sexually comatose for years is a big turn-on for me. But this guy's problem was not a snoozing libido, it was a minuscule dick, and there was nothing in the world I could do to alter his measurements. So how could I possibly get turned on myself? More to the point, was I capable of *pretending* a two-inch pecker got me hot? "I can keep myself from laughing," I said. "But that's about all I can guarantee."

"Look, I've given this a lot of thought, Lydia. And here's what I came up with."

Sylvie swiveled around in her chair, lifted a shoebox-size box from her bookshelf, swiveled back, and placed the container on her desk between us. Then she opened it and withdrew two anatomically correct plastic dolls, a male and a female. The male doll, I noticed, had an anatomically correct hard-on. I wondered if the folks in R&D at Mattel had seen this pair; heaven knows, it was high time they gave Ken and Barbie complete sets of equipment instead of those shiny blank spaces between their legs that gave me nightmares when I was a little girl. Sylvie laid Labial Barbie on her side, right leg straight, left leg bent, then placed Erectile Ken on his side between her legs.

"Maximum penetration," Sylvie announced proudly.

"Sure, if I was a seven-inch-tall plastic doll."

"Listen, Lydia, if you don't want to do this—"

"I'll do it, I'll do it," I said. What can I say? Fifteen hundred dollars makes a bang-up bequest to Paddy's ministry.

The next evening, I opened my apartment door to Raphael Matteus de Bornos-Llargos. I was thirty years old and I experienced my very first swoon. Raphael was by far the most glorious-looking specimen of the human male I had ever seen— or have seen since. His eyes were sea green and hypnotically intense; he had glowing olive skin; pronounced, high cheekbones; and long, silky-black hair. He was six-foot-three and had the body of a Greek god.

But my dazzled reaction depressed the poor guy. He froze in my doorway, his eyes cast down, his mouth tightening grimly.

It wasn't hard to figure out what he was feeling: He undoubtedly *always* had this effect on women, but *he* could foresee that the light would go out of their eyes when he debriefed.

"You are so gorgeous," I blurted out, "I wouldn't care if you didn't have a dick at all!"

It was exactly what I was thinking, but I couldn't believe I'd said it. Now *I* froze, wondering if he was going to run past me and jump out of my window. Raphael raised his luminous eyes and gazed at me, his mouth still clenched. And then, very tentatively, he smiled.

"No dick at all, eh?" he said.

"None. Zero. A blank."

"You are making a bad joke with me."

"With your looks, a penis would be too much of a good thing. Gilding the lily."

"The lily?" Raphael looked apprehensive again.

"Would you mind coming in and closing the door? Let's continue this conversation in private," I said.

Raphael entered, but remained just a couple feet inside the door. Up close, I saw that calling him an Adonis was undue flattery of the gods.

"Anyway," I said, "penises are overrated." Okay, I was gilding the lily a bit myself, but my impulse was pure.

"I do not believe you know what you are talking about," Raphael said.

"Try me."

"How do I try you?"

"A kiss would be nice."

"And then what?"

"And then I would like to spend about two hours undressing you," I said. "Very, very slowly."

"To save the insult for last," Raphael said miserably.

I hesitated a moment, then decided to stick with the truth. "There's always that possibility," I said. "I guess that's a chance we'll both have to take."

Now Raphael hesitated. He made a half-turn back toward the door, then hesitated again. What an incredible profile the man had! Michaelangelo would have drooled. I took two quick steps toward Raphael and cupped my right hand between his legs. Instantly, he was rock hard. All two inches of him. I did not laugh. I did not even smile. If that is all this dreamboat had, I'd take it.

And Raphael immediately sensed that I meant what my hand said.

"What the fuck do you think you're doing?" I snapped at Raphael as soon as his hand released my mouth.

"I am saving you," Raphael replied.

"Why don't I feel like I am being saved?" I said. I pushed him to the other side of the seat.

"Because you are frightened, perhaps?" Raphael said. *Is that what he was hoping for?*

"Raphael, you aren't going to hurt me, are you?"

"Never!"

"Are you going to kill me?"

"I would kill my mother first."

"*Are* you going to kill your mother?"

"You are making bad jokes again."

"Then why are you kidnapping me, Raffy?" There was not a doubt in my mind it was to keep me quiet about something.

What did I really know about Raphael, other than he was the firstborn son of one of the largest landowners in Argentina? That he had been a sensitive and artistic child, characteristics his father found severely lacking in *machismo,* and therefore, when Raffy told his father he wanted to live in New York, the old man was more than willing to send him off and out of sight with a sizable allowance. I am not sure if Father knew about his son's penile deficiency, but he had tried more than once to cart teenage Raffy off to a house of ill repute. Dad probably thought his son was gay, a *maricon de playa,* but I don't know whether he thought that was better or worse than a son with a pecker *muy diminuto.* What I did know was, whatever Raphael lacked, he was passionately heterosexual.

But what, exactly, did Raphael do with himself between our weekly sessions?

He would sometimes mention he was thinking of opening an art gallery, but as far as I could tell, nothing had ever come of that. He occasionally rescheduled his visits because he needed to fly off to Madrid or Paris or even, once, Morocco, to take care of some mysterious business deal. I had never given that much thought before, but now, locked inside a speeding limo, I most certainly did. Just what *were* those sudden intercontinental jaunts all about? Raphael had been the only one of my clients Sergeant Wilson had been unable to track down.

Had he been giving Wilson the slip? And was he now going to make sure that I would be permanently unable to aid the authorities in tracking him down?

"What do you want from me, Raffy?" I said. I considered the option of opening the door and flinging myself onto the highway.

"I say this is for your safety and it is true, Lydia," Raphael said. "You are an expert on so many things. Important, human things, like love and sex. But on safety, I am the expert."

"But what are you saving me *from*?"

"From jail," Raphael said. "From the police. From disappearing."

"We aren't in Argentina, Raphael. The police don't *disappear* people here."

"Are you saying that people in America do not end up in jail for bad reasons?"

Good question.

"I am saying, Raphael, that if *you* have something to hide, I won't tell the police a thing."

Raphael furrowed his spendid brow, in the process confirming a long-standing suspicion of mine: He plucked his eyebrows.

"What could I possibly have to hide?" Raphael said.

"I don't know," I said. "You're a passionate man. Maybe some of those passions became unruly."

"Unruly?" Raphael repeated, smiling boyishly. Raphael's limited grasp of the English language is one of his charms for me: I have a weakness for men who need me to educate them.

"Passions can get out of hand," I said. "And make you do things you would not do in a less passionate frame of mind."

"That is definitely true, my Lydia," Raphael said with undisguised pride.

Oh my God, was Raphael confessing to me? I had refurbished his sexual self-esteem by relieving him of his virginity, and I had managed to give him what he had been most longing for: his *machismo.* Now that he could finally do "it," he could do everything else a real man does. Like stab a rival lover to death?

I looked into Raphael's tender eyes again. He may be hypnotically beautiful, but in the end, his heart is transparent. A rare alliance, that—beauty *and* openness. Maybe one needs a tragic flaw, like a shortchanged penis, to combine the two. I found it extremely hard to believe that he was a murderer.

But wasn't that Amy's very point? Believing that someone you know and care about is a murderer is world-shattering. When the evident truth and your heart's desire come into conflict, it's a lose-lose situation. It creates a kind of emotional dissonance. I was reminded of one of Sylvie's jokes, from back in her Barnard days when she still had a sense of humor: A guy comes home to find his best friend in bed with his wife. Incredibly, the best friend protests his innocence. In his last-ditch plea, this friend says, "Listen, pal, what are you going to believe—me or your eyes?"

"You killed him for me, Raphael?" I asked softly. *Where was a tape recorder when you really needed one?*

Raphael hesitated for a moment, then said, "No, it is not me who needs to hide. It is you I am worried about."

"Me?"

"Yes, my friend. You, who I owe so very much."

"Why worry about me? You killed him, not me," I said.

"But I did not kill him, Lydia. I thought that you did."

Good grief, it was déjà-Frank all over again!

"Raphael, I did not kill Michael Linscott."

"I would not care if you had. You would have your reasons and I would accept them."

"But I *didn't*."

"Then I believe you."

"I'm glad to hear that."

"But the police believe you did. And that is a big problem," Raphael said.

The limo driver turned onto Route 80 West.

"The police aren't sure who did it. Not yet," I said. "They are still investigating."

"Listen to me, Lydia. If they do not *discover* who did it, they will *decide* who did it. This is the way the police work in every country. They need to arrest someone. And that some-one will be you."

The same theory of police work that both Abe and Paddy had proposed just yesterday.

"Where are you taking me, Raphael?"

"To Casablanca."

I laughed. "You're joking."

"I have a house there. You will be safe. We will have a good life."

"Raphael, you are absolutely crazy!" I said. Actually, I was feeling wonderfully giddy just then. Outside the car window I saw a sign flash by: TETERBORO AIRPORT—5 MILES.

"The plane is waiting. Everything is in order," Raphael said.

Did I detect a touch of Bogart in his delivery?

"Just fly off to Casablanca and start a new life," I murmured. Substitute Paris, and that was what Michael had had in mind. *What is it about men wanting to make casual pleasures permanent?*

"Extraordinary times require extraordinary actions," Raphael said. The line sounded rehearsed and I loved him for it.

"But to run away when I am not guilty—"

"That makes it even more honorable," Raphael said.

His was the kind of Romance-language logic that always enthralled me as a French major, but never really made any sense.

We were entering the airport, heading for a hangar identified as BUSINESS ALLIANCE PARTNERS. Just beyond the hangar, I could see a Lear 25 with its lights on and door opened. Our getaway jet.

I looked at Raphael. Gorgeous, terrifyingly gorgeous. If I were to say that I had never dreamed of starting life over in some exotic realm with a beautiful and adoring man, I would be perjuring myself. I don't think there is a woman in America who has not indulged in this reverie at least once. And *Casablanca*, no less! *Making passionate love on a filigree-curtained feather bed, while a snake charmer plays his flute outside the open window* . . . So, Lydia, what will it be? What are you really made of? When push comes to shove, is it true what they say in Brooklyn—that you can take the girl out of Flatbush, but you can't take Flatbush out of the girl?

The limousine came to a stop in front of the hangar. The chauffeur, a skinny man in livery, jumped out and opened the door on my side. I did not move.

"The plane is waiting," Raphael said softly.

Suddenly I had a vivid vision of Homicide Captain Amy Liu walking out of her Sherry-Netherland hotel room with her husband, Barry, in tow. Amy's face was impassive, but I could detect an expression of stoic resignation in her eyes. That look said, "Beware of what you desire, Lydia, for you will surely get it."

"I'm sorry, Raffy. Can't do it," I said.

"Please."

"You are the most wonderful man I know," I said, putting my hands on both sides of his face. "And God knows, you've come through for me in all of this the way no one else has. But I have to see this thing through here."

He pulled back and my hands fell away from his face.

"It . . . it is because of . . ." Raffy gestured toward his crotch. "Because of *this*, is it not so?"

"Of course not!" The volume and vehemence of my words came as a surprise even to me. And to sensitive, intelligent, *damaged* Raphael Matteus de Bornos-Llargos, they were a dagger in the heart. *The lady doth protest too much*, and we both knew it. In my defining existential moment, my choice was, No, I do not want to spend the rest of my life with a man who has a two-inch penis. Not even in Casablanca. At that moment, I absolutely detested myself for being so insipidly human.

We drove back to Manhattan in silence.

17

Paddy was standing by the window with his back to me when I let myself in, and when he turned around, I saw he had been crying. I ran to him and threw my arms around him. Instantly, I was weeping too. We stood for several minutes, our heads pressed against one another's shoulders. All the betrayals of the past three days—both *of* me and *by* me came pouring out. I knew that whatever happened, my life would never be the same.

"I just can't bear it anymore," Paddy said finally.

"I know," I whispered.

"I loved him like a brother," Paddy said. He let go of me and walked to the coffee table, where he'd left a tumbler and a bottle of Scotch.

"*Michael?*"

"Manuel," Paddy said.

He refilled his glass, then pointed to another by way of asking me if I wanted a drink too. I did, I nodded.

"There is something so incredibly Christlike about him, isn't there?" Paddy went on. "The way he embraces his poverty, makes it a virtue. He never took a penny from me. Did you know that? He wouldn't even take an extra portion of beef jerky, for God's sake."

"What happened?" I said.

Paddy handed me my glass of Scotch and we sat down. "I went by to pick him up in the truck," he said. "Thursday, right? We service the overflow at the Bowery Mission."

I nodded.

"Anyway, I always pick him up at the entrance to Chelsea Piers. He's easy to spot, especially in summer when he wears his Pink Floyd T-shirt." Paddy drained his glass. "But he wasn't there. I waited for a while, then double-parked. They may have taken away my credentials for administering communion, but I'm still allowed to prop up my CLERGY ON CALL sign. Pretty good trade-off."

This was one of Paddy's running gags. Obviously, his story was about to take a turn for the worse and he wasn't ready to go there yet. "So I dropped by Manuel's house—'32 Dumpster Place,' as he calls it. He's even got a little mailbox in front with that painted on it. He thinks it's a homey touch. And it is." Paddy stared into his empty glass before he continued. "I called to him, but didn't get an answer. I got worried then. What if he was sick? Nobody would ever see him inside that thing. So I climbed up the box steps and looked in. He wasn't home." Paddy began to tear up again.

"Go on, Paddy."

"He's got it all set up in there. A threadbare easy chair, a table with a transistor radio. A mattress, blanket, wash basin, bottles of water. Even pictures—cut-outs from magazines. And then he's got his shelf of knickknacks. The same dumb stuff my mother collects." Paddy took a long breath. "In fact, several of them looked just like my mother's figurines. And they were, Lydia. They *were* my mother's."

"What are you talking about?"

"I climbed inside and looked. Four of them were my mother's. Her holy lamb set."

"Her what?"

"It's this little girl and a lamb. One's called 'Beside Still Waters' and another's called 'No Tears Past the Gate.'"

"Paddy, they hardly sound like one-of-a-kind items. Your mother and Manuel probably have the same awful taste—"

"My mother's were stolen three weeks ago," Paddy said. "She told me yesterday when I dropped by. They went missing the same day I brought Manuel home to meet her. She wasn't going to mention it to me."

"So Manuel stole some stupid figurines. So he's not a saint after all—"

"There were some other items that went missing that day," Paddy said. "Like her wooden-handled ice pick."

"My God."

"Yes, my God, indeed," Paddy said sorrowfully. "I called Sergeant Wilson and I asked him if I could have a closer look at the murder weapon. He said it could be arranged. I met him at the precinct and he took me downtown to where they store evidence. The ice pick is my mother's."

"How could you tell?"

"I remembered it clearly. My dad won it as a door prize about twenty years ago at a bar that used to be in the neighborhood. Kedding's Bar and Grille. That's what it says on the handle of the murder weapon."

"It could be a coincidence."

"The *l*'s in 'Grille' were faded, I remember that too. So it looked like it said, 'Kedding's Bar and Griii.' It was the same one, Lydia. And he does have a key to our apartment."

I started to cry. For a few minutes, the two of us simply sat there, facing one another, Scotch glasses in hand, weeping together again. So it turned out to be just the opposite of what the *Post* thought it was—*hoped* that it was. Not a sexy crime of the rich and famous, not a murder that could be dignified by calling it a crime of passion, but the same old, same old—a senseless murder by a crazy homeless man. A crime born of poverty, not of passion. But I would be lying if I did not say that I was crying from relief too. The awful drama was over. I was off the hook.

"So you told Wilson?" I asked.

"I had to," Paddy said. "Not because of their laws, but God's. Not that it makes a difference to Manuel. They found him and he confessed. He said he stole the ice pick from my mother's and then murdered Michael with it. He's in jail now. It turns out he has quite a record. Wilson is going to let me talk to him. I'm going down there first thing in the morning, but I wanted to tell you about it first."

"But *why*, Paddy? Why did he kill Michael?"

"Who knows? I guess I didn't really know him. What tortures his soul."

"Did he know what I did in here? You know, with Michael. And with the others?"

"Yes. He once asked me where the money for our ministry came from and I told him."

"So maybe it was that?" I guessed. "Some kind of moral outrage? Not even the underclass is immune from that."

"You may be right." Now Paddy stood, walked to me, and kneeled down in front of me. He took one of my hands and held it in both of his. "I have never been ashamed of what you do, Lydia," he said, looking up into my eyes.

Reflexively, I yanked my hand away from his.

I cannot say precisely why I resented Paddy so much just then. Perhaps after my sad interlude with Raphael, he was the proverbial straw that broke this camel's back. It was not that Paddy sounded patronizing. It was just the very concept that he *might* feel shame for the way I earned my keep . . . and his . . . and the keep of his indigent charges.

"What's wrong?" Paddy said.

"I don't know. You just seem like such a fucking *priest* right now."

"I am a priest, Lydia!"

"Then go see Manuel. Beg *his* forgiveness and save *his* soul. But don't you dare think of forgiving *me* for anything!"

"Lydia, please!"

I got up and bolted to my bedroom.

18

I must have lain on my floor bawling my eyes out for a good twenty minutes before I finally fell asleep. It was ten in the morning before I awoke. My first thought was that the closed-circuit NYPD-TV was probably still in place and my goodnight monologue of tears had been watched and recorded.

I got up off the floor and stood directly in front of my dresser mirror. They'd probably hid their camera behind that, right? Just like in the police interrogation room. "And so ends today's episode of reality TV's biggest hit, *Fucked!*" I intoned to my closed-circuit audience. "Will Lydia Quess ever be happy again? Will she get her courtesan pride back? Who knows? Tune in tomorrow, *assholes!*" I gave the mirror the finger and pirouetted away. Then, with my back to the mirror, I looked coyly over my shoulder and said, "You were expecting some hot stuff, weren't you? Sorry to disappoint."

The phone rang.

It was probably the NYPD begging for a shimmy at the very least.

I let it ring a few times, then walked downstairs to pick it up in the kitchen. Paddy wasn't home. "Yes?" I said listlessly into the phone.

"You've heard, of course," was the greeting. It was Sylvia.

"About Manuel?"

"Yes. Awful, isn't it?" She did not attempt to camouflage her relief. Her voice bordered on gleeful. The case had been solved with nary a mention of her in the press; her thriving practice was home free.

"Yes, it is awful," I said, my voice flat.

"Well, I'm glad for all of us that this is finally over," Sylvie went on blithely. "But just to be on the cautious side, I don't think I'll be making any referrals to you for a while. Just let this wind down first and then see where we stand."

"Is that why you called?"

"Basically," she said. "And to see how you are doing. I know this has put a strain on our relationship and I'm sorry about that, you know."

It was an apology, and the decent thing to do would have been to accept it—at the very least, acknowledge it. But I was unable to do that.

"Good-bye, Sylvia," I said.

"Lydia?"

"Yes?"

"I'm sure Michael told you about our plans."

She said it so casually, I realized immediately that she was fishing. "Of course," I said. Of course, I did not have the faintest idea what she was talking about.

"Well, we're going to have to wait a suitable interval for that too," Sylvia said. "But I just wanted you to know that Prassad and I won't forget about you."

"I appreciate that."

"Take care," Sylvia said and she hung up.

Prassad and I won't forget about you? I opened the refrigerator and instantly slipped into my usual open-fridge trance: Leftover Chinese take-out? Apricot juice? Prosciutto? *What in the name of God had Sylvie been talking about?* I was still chewing over this—and a shrimp roll— when Paddy came home. I had never seen him look so desolate, and it broke my heart. "Paddy," I said. "I am sorry for what I said. I know how awful this is for you."

He did not reply.

I followed him into the living room, where he curled up like a child on the couch, his face turned away from me. I sat on the end of the couch.

"He says that he does not know why he does anything anymore," Paddy whispered. "He believes the devil crept into his soul one night while he was sleeping in his Dumpster. He says the devil is stronger than he is."

In one of our late-night, Scotch-on-the-rocks seminars, Paddy and I concluded that of all the Bible's dangerous lessons, the notion of a devil who battles God for men's souls is surely the most treacherous. It robs men of their will and, in the process, of their dignity. What is more, once the devil got entangled in the popular mind with Freud's ultimate goofiness, the unconscious, civilization was doomed to an endless litany of, "The devil made me do it!" It was all downhill from there.

But this was not a late-night exercise in philosophy. It was Paddy's dear friend's life, unique and final.

"I hope you could comfort him," I said.

"He barely remembers doing it," Paddy said. Then he whispered, "I'm going back to El Salvador."

Oh no, I had been afraid of this ever since he had told me about Manuel's guilt. It was probably the real reason I had gotten so angry at him last night. "What about your people here?" I protested. "They depend on you."

"They don't depend on anybody," Paddy said, turning around to face me. His cheeks were red, his eyes cold. "That's why they are where they are."

These were the most uncharitable words I had ever heard Paddy utter and he knew it too. He suddenly swung his feet off the couch and stood. "I need to pray," he said. "Badly."

"I can understand that."

"In church."

"Sounds like a good place."

A minute later he was out the door again, his face warped with grief. And a minute after that, I took the elevator down to the vestibule. Agron was at his post.

"I am thinking about you," he said.

"Happy thoughts?"

"I am happy this murder case is revealed," he said. "I see about it on TV this morning."

"But I bet it hasn't changed people's opinion of me in the building, has it?"

Agron examined the tips of his old world shoes. "No, it does not seem to be so," he said.

"How about yours?"

"My opinion of you never changes, Mrs. Quess," he said. "That is because I can see beyond your outside into your inside."

"How does it look in there?"

"Pure and clean."

"As compared to my outside?"

Agron blushed.

"Listen, Agron, could you spare me a few minutes? I need some help in my apartment."

"I come soon quickly," Agron said. "My coffee break is in ten minutes."

By the time Agron knocked on my door, I had located my *Learning to Love Again* tape in our living room bookcase. It had slipped behind a row of books along with *French Cooking for Beginners,* a book I'd bought for Paddy last Christmas to no evident effect. I inserted the tape into the VCR and pressed "FAST FORWARD."

"Come in," I called. "I'm in the living room."

Agron barely looked at me as he walked in. His eyes were glued to the television screen where Danny Bloomster and his costar were flipping and jerking around on the bed at high

speed. I was about to explain to Agron that it was even more
hilarious at normal speed, when he said, "Do not make me
ashamed, Mrs. Quess."

"Then don't look at it," I replied, more tartly than I should
have. I guess I was still smarting from my unanswered question about the comparative looks of my outsides and insides.
The tape had come to near its end, with Danny and Barbie
symmetrically patting each other's genitalia—in fast forward,
it looked like they were tapping out Morse Code. I pressed
"PLAY," then "PAUSE." Arrested on the screen was the tasteful
logo for The Kahn-Panaik Institute, the Medusa medical em-
blem of two snakes coiled like DNA around a central staff, but
for its head, one of these snakes sported the female Venus
symbol, while the other was crowned with the male Mars
symbol. Next to the logo, just as I had remembered, was an
artful photograph of Doctors Kahn and Panaik, her seated,
him standing behind her with a hand on her shoulder. Their
faces exuded solicitousness.

"You can look now, Agron," I said. "Have you ever seen either of those people before?"

Agron nodded. "Both," he said.

"Where?"

"At the Roof Dining Room."

"The Yale Club."

"Yes."

"Were they with anybody else you recognized?" No leading
of the witness allowed.

"Yes."

"Who, Agron?"

"The dead man," he said.

Bingo!

"With long business papers?" I said.

Agron nodded.

"Arguing?"

"Pounding the table," Agron said.

"Thank you, Agron."

"That is the help you ask me for?"

"Yes."

Agron started to ask me a question, then stopped.

"What's up, Agron?" I said.

"It is not my business," he said.

"We are friends," I said. "So whatever it is, it is the business of both of us."

After a long moment he asked, "Why have you made sex with Rico?"

"Rico?"

"Rico. Waiter at Yale Club." Agron looked over my shoulder into the middle distance, girding himself for my reply.

So I had been right. That boy who let me into Michael's secret room had not been constrained by historical fact. He had told all of his fellow waiters about the rambunctious sex he had enjoyed with this hot and hungry visitor in one of the residence rooms. Someone put two and two together and produced my snazzy photograph on the cover of the *Post*. A match. Enter Agron.

"I never made sex with Rico," I said. *"Never."*

I do not believe I have ever seen Agron look happier. "He was lying?"

"Through his teeth," I said.

"I believed this was so always," Agron said. He stood there in front of me, his oversized grin creasing his oversized face. I stood on my tiptoes and planted a kiss on the tip of his nose.

"I'm holding out for someone taller," I whispered.

Sometimes I just cannot help myself.

19

If anything, Amy Liu had underestimated Google's powers of detection.

First, I made a list of terms—"Michael Linscott," "Sylvia Kahn," "Sylvia Panaik," "Prassad Panaik," "Kahn-Panaik Institute," "Limited Corporations," "C Corporation," "S Corporation," "Limited Liabilities Companies," "Proprietorships," "Partnerships," "Registered Copyright," and "Tax Identification Number"—then plugged them into my computer in pairs, using every possible permutation. I got dozens of hits, but none of them led me anywhere interesting. Then, on a hunch, I added "Learning to Love Again" to the list, ran the combos, and hit the jackpot.

Learning to Love Again had been copyrighted.

And not just as an "educational film," but as the corporate name of a new S corporation in the state of Delaware. From there, it was a cyber-hop to this new corporation's Federal Tax Identification Number, registered one week ago. This, in turn, led directly to its principals, Linscott and Panaik. And from there, by routing myself through Baker Library at the Harvard Business School (the most valuable piece of information I remember from my tenure in Cambridge is my six-digit Baker access code), I was back in Delaware, reading Learning to Love Again Corp's "statement of principal business activity." It was "nationally franchising sex therapy clinics and innovative therapeutic procedures for marital happiness."

Huh?

What the hell kind of franchise was that?

I mean, what did Sylvia have to offer her franchisees other than *Learning to Love Again,* the movie? Anybody with a mini-cam could produce a film as fetching as that one; hell, they could probably get Paris Hilton to star in it. Everything else in her practice, Sylvia had lifted straight from Masters and Johnson, and in three weeks flat, at that. There was nothing stopping anybody else from doing the same.

Perhaps it was branding. Like "Midas Mufflers" or, more to the point, the Boston Medical Group, that chain of one-stop shopping clinics that offer men a total of fifty different medications for getting a hard-on. Those folks had actually trademarked the phrase "Sex for life!" Name recognition is everything these days. So "Learning to Love Again" could become a national name brand, complete with sophisticated advertising.

But did your local sex therapist in, say, Des Moines or Duluth, really *need* a brand name and a national ad campaign to drum up business? Sylvia had had her practice up and running at full capacity in a month's time with none of that. And why would Sylvie and Prassad need an investment banker of Michael's stature to launch this enterprise? You could probably set up the whole deal with less than a hundred grand and LegalZoom.com.

Unless . . .

Where was the *real* money in all of this?

The surrogates, of course! The *big* money came from the surrogates and the commissions they generated. And not merely the commission for the therapists' patient referrals, but the commission for continued services *after* the patients stopped seeing the therapist. *That* was a gift that just kept on giving. An annuity that multiplied with each new patient the therapist saw and referred to a surrogate. Because in the end, Sylvia clearly *did* know what Teodora di Sebastiano had known and counted upon: Once a patient got hooked on a surrogate, that surrogate was in business for the long haul. In the final analysis, Sylvia made oodles more money from patients who did *not* transfer their erotic sensibilities back home. Hey, Amy had more or less figured that out the first time I met her.

Now *that* was an idea worth franchising.

With clinics in every major city from Bangor to Seattle, the surrogate business and its everlasting annuities from graduate patients would be the centerpiece of Learning to Love Again™. What Starbucks had done for coffee, Doctors Panaik and Khan would do for sex. Yes, indeed, they had come up with an idea in a million: how to legalize prostitution nationally.

And how to make it their very own monopoly.

By golly, it was the American dream come true.

And then it hit me: It was not Sylvia and Prassad who had come up with the idea of going national. It was Michael. Michael Peabody Linscott III, the man who prided himself on seeing the big picture, the man who kept a secret venture office at the Yale Club, the man whose last words to me were that he had a megadeal brewing that would set us free to shop until we dropped in Parisian antique book shops. Michael had experienced firsthand what Sylvia's innovative therapeutic procedures for marital happiness could do for him—terrific sex with another woman for as long as he could afford it. Franchising this procedure would spread the joy and make him financially independent.

In college, I took a course in moral reasoning. Actually, I chose the course on Sylvia's recommendation. The professor was a pear-shaped woman in her fifties with a treacherous imagination. She would start every class with her most recently concocted scenario of a morally dicey situation. Like, "If you surgically implant the button that launches the hydrogen bomb inside an innocent man's chest, and the President has to cut that man open with his own hands to start a nuclear war, would the President have a clearer grasp of the moral consequences of his act?" We were supposed to come away from these classes with a heightened respect for analytic reasoning, plus the moral imperative to think through every ethical choice from every conceivable angle. I often came away from these classes thinking that the really difficult choices are invariably lose-lose situations, so why even ponder them?

In the end, it all basically comes down to choosing your poison.

"I've got good news and I've got good news," Amy said as she sashayed through my door with a smile.

"I'll take the good news first," I said.

"Okay, I've come to apologize to you." With these words, she produced a bag of Krispy Kreme doughnuts from behind her back.

"Yum," I said. "Doughnuts accepted. But what's the apology for?"

"Suspecting you of murder."

"It's your job," I said. "I think these would go nicely with a cappuccino, don't you?"

"No, I mean *really* suspecting you," Amy said, looking me straight in the eyes. "Enough to have a warrant for your arrest completely filled out and ready to go at ten o'clock last night."

"On second thought, how about a buttered rum espresso?" I said.

"Sounds good to me," Amy said.

She followed me into the kitchen, where I lined up my ingredients: nutmeg, butter, rum, espresso beans. I stared at them a moment, then turned around and said, "Okay, now I'll take the good news."

"You're rich," Amy said. "A millionaire, if the Euro keeps holding its own against the dollar."

The Swiss bank account! Amy had found out about it.

"So that's what made you think I did it," I said. "If I killed Michael, I'd get to keep it all for myself. And nobody would ever know about the money or where it came from."

"Exactly," Amy said. "I mean, let's face it, Lydia, you were always a suspect. You had to be. He was killed in your bed. Your prints were all over his body, including some bloody prints from after he was stabbed. And we couldn't place anyone but you at the scene of the crime. All that was missing was a motive. I mean, other than self-defense, and you didn't bite on that."

"Because it wasn't true."

"Obviously. At least now, it's obvious," Amy went on. "But then last night one of my people searched Linscott's room at the Yale Club. He found your joint Swiss bank account in one of his file cabinets. He also found Linscott's petition for divorce."

"Let me get this straight—you actually thought that added up to enough to indict me for *murder*?"

"Not only did we, so did the DA," Amy said.

"That stinks!" I howled. "The whole bloody system stinks. You could have sent an innocent person to jail!"

"I know," Amy said, shaking her head. "Thank God, Manuel confessed when he did."

"You're a shit, Amy! You're no friend of mine!" I said. I meant it.

"Please, Lydia. I told you I came to apologize," Amy said. "Manuel confessed less than an hour after I filled out your warrant. I can't tell you how happy it made me to rip that thing up. You were innocent! We really could be friends."

She reached out to touch my shoulder, but I stepped away from her.

"Too late," I said. "You can keep your doughnuts. And while you're at it, you can keep Michael's money too. It's blood money. I don't want it."

Amy stood there in front of me, her face wrenched with what looked for all the world like anguish. "This isn't easy for me," she said softly. "I didn't have to tell you any of this, you know. I just felt I needed to, so we could start fresh. I am begging you to forgive me, Lydia."

I believe that in another moment or two I might have forgiven Amy. I *was* running low on friends. Drastically low. But the truth is, I will never know for sure if I would have made peace with Amy Liu in my kitchen just then because the phone rang. I picked it up before it rang a second time, mostly because it gave me an excuse to look away from Amy's beseeching eyes.

"Hello?"

"I'd like to speak with Paddy."

"He's out right now. Is this Mrs. Riordin?"

"Yes."

"Paddy went to church, Mrs. Riordin. He needed to pray."

"Well, at least some good has come of all this," Mrs. Riordin replied.

"Can I give him a message?"

"Just tell him to call his mother as soon as possible."

"Listen, Mrs. Riordin, he's probably at Our Lady of Pompeii. That's his favorite church in our neighborhood. What do you want me to tell him?"

There was a pause long enough to recite at least two Hail Marys. I looked over at Amy. She was staring at the unopened bag of doughnuts on my kitchen table. Sure, she was anguished, but she was probably hungry too. I, of all people, know for a fact that those two feelings can coexist.

"It's about that Spanish boy, Manuel," Mrs. Riordin said.

"Yes?" I said.

"I knew there was something wrong with him the minute I saw him. It's in his eyes, you know. You can't hide those things. You cannot hide a craven heart. That boy was capable of anything."

I sighed. "What is it that you want me to tell your son, Mrs. Riordin?"

"The papers said that boy murdered the man with an ice pick he stole from our house," Mrs. Riordin began. "Well, I don't know if it makes any difference, except to Mr. Riordin and myself, of course, but Mr. Riordin tells me that he couldn't have stole it from our house because we didn't have it here. Paddy's father packed it up with Paddy's things when Paddy moved out to Manhattan. Because it had always been a favorite of Paddy's. Since he was a little boy. He always did like old-fashioned things, you know. And we had no use for it—we've had an automatic defrost for years."

Yes! "Mrs. Riordin?" I said hurriedly.

"Yes?"

"Don't tell anybody else about this, will you? I think Paddy should hear about it first."

Mrs. Riordin said fine, and hung up.

I hung up too and looked at Amy. It did not appear that she had picked up anything suspicious-sounding from my end of the phone conversation. And she had not given in and opened up the Krispy Kreme bag; the lady had a sense of decorum. I, however, was feeling a tremendous sense of urgency. If Amy had been ready to arrest me for Michael's murder before Manuel confessed, she would be right back in her office filling out a new warrant the moment she heard that Manuel's confession turned out to have a *major* discrepancy in it.

"I need some time to think about all this, Amy," I lied.

"I can understand that."

"And for what it's worth, I never knew Michael was filing for divorce." That was a fact, but the only reason I mentioned it was to toss a little more guilt in Amy's direction. Give her something to wallow in while I got my ass in gear.

"Well, I guess you're the last to hear then. His wife knew, she'd already seen her lawyer. And she knew about that Swiss bank account too—it's in her countersuit." Amy shook her head. "What a guy that Linscott was, eh? His wife was the one with most of the money, you know. Until Linscott poured the bulk of it into his investment schemes. And then he was going to divorce her on grounds of infidelity. *Her* infidelity. With Danny Bloomster. At least Mrs. Linscott comes out of it with some insurance money. Plus her husband's investments, for whatever they're worth."

Amy meant this torrent of police *intelligence-qua-gossip* as a kind of peace offering, a substitute for all the information she had withheld from me all along. Yet I also heard in it a trace of disapproval for my role in Michael Linscott's short life; after all, I was the beneficiary of his ill-gotten gains. But maybe I was being overly sensitive. I've been known to get that way when I am being devious.

I got Amy out of my apartment—without her bag of doughnuts—as fast as I could. Then I ran up to Paddy's room and into his closet. Sure enough, there were still seven cardboard boxes there, all taped shut. His mother had labeled each of the boxes with a black marker: PADDY'S HIGH SCHOOL TROPHIES; PADDY'S CLOTHES—OLD; PADDY'S CLOTHES—NEW; PADDY'S FAVORITES, etc. PADDY'S FAVORITES looked as if it might have been opened and then taped shut again. "A favorite of Paddy's"—the exact words Mrs. Riordin had used to describe the ice pick.

I opened the FAVORITES box and dumped the contents on the closet floor. Every item had been wrapped in paper towels and Scotch-taped closed. I squatted down and unwrapped them one at a time. It was quite a collection: an old Sears manual haircutting kit; a bamboo tray decorated with a pastel portrait of Popeye; a desktop barometer; a deck of playing cards with pictures on the backs of young women in bulky swimwear. This last was a 1980s Brooklyn Catholic boy's idea of pornography; what had Mrs. Riordin been thinking when she wrapped them up? As I expected, there was not an ice pick in sight.

I was packing up the box again when a glint of light caught my eye. It came from between two of the unopened boxes. I pulled one of those boxes away from the closet wall; the glinting object spun to the floor and stuck in, blade first. A knife. A serrated tomato knife. The kind that hangs in knife racks over kitchen stoves, right between the bread knife and the paring knife. If I was not mistaken, the very position on Danny Bloomster's knife rack that had been vacant. Not only were Amy and her crew of detectives full of shit when it came to contriving murder theories, there were also incompetent in the field! *Two-plus days* searching my apartment and they hadn't turned up this knife!?

Of course, it was not *the* murder weapon—that had been an ice pick.

So maybe Amy's crew *had* found the knife, maybe even tested it for fingerprints, but nothing had come of it, so they put it back. All because they were thinking inside the box, so to speak.

But it all fit together for me. Perfectly. The murderer had been hiding in Paddy's closet while Michael and I made love in the next room. The murderer found the ice pick in Paddy's box of favorite things and realized it was a more suitable instrument for the task at hand. What was more, it had the added advantage of offering the police a nice bit of misdirection; it would tie the weapon to our apartment—to me, for example. So the murderer abandoned his knife in the closet, and took the ice pick into my bedroom to pierce Michael Linscott's heart.

That abandoned knife belonged to Danny Bloomster.

Bloomster was the killer.

Oh, you need a powerful motive, Captain Liu? How about a brand-new, 300-seat theater?

And what about Manuel's confession? He probably wasn't the first guilt-addled homeless man frightened into confessing to a crime that he could not remember committing. Throw in the fact that Manuel idolized Paddy, a man of God, and that this man of God had been the one to accuse him of murder, and you've got a guilt-addled homeless man who believes not only that he *must* have committed the crime, but that the Devil made him do it.

Five minutes later, I was standing in front of my apartment building, clutching a small paper bag. To my left, about five blocks away, was Our Lady of Pompeii, where I was sure I could find Paddy. If I went there right now, I could tell him his mother's entire story and relieve his tormented soul. But then Paddy would insist on going to the police, on immediately talking with Manuel. Straight ahead, about twenty blocks away, was The Loft Playhouse, whose artistic director had left an outgoing message on his answering machine that he would be in rehearsal at the theater all day. No matter what I did, I probably had an hour at best before Mrs. Riordin related her story to someone else, someone who would tell the police or the press or both. The clock was ticking.

Tick, tock.

Lose, lose.

Choose your poison.

I flagged a cab and gave the driver the address for The Loft Playhouse.

20

Danny Bloomster was declaiming from the far end of a third-floor loft on Hester Street in Chinatown. My entrance via the stairwell had gone easily unnoticed, in large part because of the din of sewing machines. The Loft Playhouse shared its space with a small sweatshop that appeared to be producing knockoffs of Lacoste polo shirts. Bloomster had moved on to another Pacino favorite, *Richard III*.

> *"And therefore, since I cannot prove a lover*
> *To entertain these fair well-spoken days,*
> *I am determined to prove a villain*
> *And hate the idle pleasures of these days."*

"Since I cannot prove a lover . . . I am determined to prove a villain"—that pretty much nailed it, didn't it? As I watched,

Bloomster was instructing his Lady Anne in how to look adoringly at him. I crept along the wall until I was no more than ten feet away from them.

"Prop girl," I announced.

Bloomster shaded his eyes against the photographer's lamp that served as the theater's sole spotlight. He still could not see me. "What?"

"The dagger, my lord. The one you hand to her in the next scene," I said, taking several quick steps closer. He saw me now.

"What the fuck—Babycakes? What the hell are you doing here?"

I withdrew the tomato knife from my paper bag and held it out straight-arm, the serrated blade only inches from Bloomster's neck. Lady Anne looked annoyed at the interruption.

"Where the hell did you find that?" Bloomster said. Apparently, he did not take my threat very seriously. Either that or he was hoping that if he played this scene persuasively enough, it would displace reality. That, I believe, is the main reason people choose the actor's life; it provides them with a virtual universe of denial.

"In Paddy's closet, where you left it," I said.

I touched the tip of the knife to Bloomster's Adam's apple. He winced. There is nothing like the prick of a knife to pierce the suspension of disbelief.

"I don't know what the fuck you're talking about," Bloomster croaked. Rather persuasively, I must say.

"Next door to my bedroom. Where you were hiding until I went downstairs the night of the murder."

"You're nuts!" Bloomster said, holding his head—and neck—up very straight. Lady Anne had backed far away.

"It's your knife. From over your stove. The missing knife."

"So, what did you do—steal it? I noticed it was gone after our little *rendezvous*."

"Bullshit," I said. My arm was getting tired and more than a little shaky. I had already drawn a dot of blood from Bloomster's neck.

"Did you take your meds today, lady?" Bloomster said.

"So you admit the knife is yours," I went on, grasping my knife arm at the elbow in order to steady it.

"Hey, it looks like mine, but I wouldn't swear to it," Bloomster said, looking seriously bewildered. If I had any doubts before, I was now sure that Bloomster did not have the wherewithal to have pulled off this murder on his own.

"In about two minutes, I am going to call the police. But first I'm going to ask you a question—who's in this with you? That pretty boy in your building? Angelica?"

Bloomster just stood there, mute. I flashed on Amy in the interrogation room of the Tenth Precinct: *It's called "mitigating circumstances," Petey. The kind judges take into account when they pass out sentences.* "It's called 'turning state's evidence,' Danny," I said. "Judges take these things into account when they pass out sentences."

Without intending to, I had emphasized the word "sentences" with a little poke of my forefinger; two more dots of blood appeared on Bloomster's neck. I was suddenly aware that the sewing machines behind me had stopped humming. Bloomster looked terrified. He did not say a word.

"It *was* Angelica who came up with the plan, wasn't it?" I said.

"Why are you obsessed with me and that bitch? She dumped me, okay?" Bloomster said. "Promised me the moon and dumped me."

"*After* you killed her husband for her."

"What? I didn't kill anybody!" Bloomster pleaded. "You're really freaking me out, lady. Would you *please* take that knife away?"

I lowered the tip to Bloomster's belly. He took this as a gesture of quasi-appeasement.

"She dumped me for that Indian asshole," Bloomster said. "The sex doctor."

"*Panaik?* Dr. Kahn's husband?"

"You can find them at the Plaza every weekday afternoon. Practicing the *karma sutra.*"

"I don't believe you."

"I followed her, for crissake! The day she gave me the kiss-off."

I believed him.

Moments later, I was in the middle of Chinatown, searching frantically for a taxi. *My kingdom for a Checker Cab . . .*

21

"Sometimes a simple caress can be much more satis-fying than an orgasm," Dr. Sylvia Kahn was crooning to a couple across from her desk as I banged into her office unannounced.

"But if you want orgasms, we've got people to take care of that for you," I said, coming alongside Sylvia's desk. The hus-band found both my reckless entrance and my impudent quip wildly amusing. But he was the only one laughing.

"Lydia!" Sylvia gasped. "This is hardly professional behavior!"

"No, I do all my professional behavior lying down," I said.

"Please, forgive this intrusion," Dr. Kahn said to the couple in haute therapy tones. "This woman has been under a great deal of stress."

"That's true," I said, smiling complicity at the wife patient. "It's because I haven't had a decent orgasm all week."

The man abruptly stopped laughing; I guess I wasn't funny to him anymore. The couple stood and headed for the door.

"No charge for this session," Sylvie called after them. "Same time next week?" They slammed the office door behind them.

"I'm calling Prassad," Sylvia said to me. "I think you need to be sedated immediately—"

"Call him where? The Plaza?" I said.

"I don't know what you are talking about."

I do not believe she did.

"I don't have a lot of time, Sylvie," I said. "Tell me about Learning to Love Again. The franchise. Fantastic idea, by the way—Michael's, right? But he drove one hell of a hard bargain, didn't he? He was going to screw you and Prassad out of a decent share." If Michael cheated Frank, it was a good bet that he did the same thing to Sylvie and Prassad. That would account for the pounding of tables at the Yale Club.

Sylvia looked both frightened of me and worried about my mental health in equal parts. I was touched by the worry, but it was the fear that was working to my advantage.

"What is wrong with you, Lydia?" she stalled.

"Just tell me!" I snapped. "And this can be painless."

"Is this about the stock options Michael promised you? I *told* you Prassad and I would honor them."

"No, this is about Michael and *you*," I said. "You never did work out your partnership with him, did you? Right up until his murder."

"They solved the goddamn murder, Lydia, remember? It's over! *Kaput!* Over and done with! I'm sure that your priest pal is not happy with how it turned out, but there you are. Manuel was crazy and he did it. Can we please get over it and get on with our lives?"

"Manuel didn't do it," I said. "The police know that now." Well, soon enough they would.

"You're in denial, Lydia."

"No, that's your department, Sylvia. Let me make this easy for you. You never finalized the partnership with Michael, but you did with his heir—with Angelica. Just a simple 'yes' or 'no' will do."

"That is none of your business," Sylvia said.

"Hey, the murder is solved—you say so yourself. So what difference does it make now?"

"Absolutely none," Sylvia said. "But it's still none of your business."

Was that a footfall in the waiting room? Sylvia obviously heard something too.

"Prassad?" she called out. The expression on Sylvia's face struck me as the look of someone who loved too much, and who knew only too well the perilousness of that condition. As for myself, I was both excited and scared to death.

No answer from the waiting room.

"Okay, let me tell you something that some people think is none of *your* business," I said. I drew in a deep breath. If Prassad was out there listening, I was about to take one hell of a risk. "I'm sorry to have to tell you this, Sylvie, but your husband is fucking Angelica. Daily. In a room they keep at the Plaza."

"You're crazy!"

"Afraid not," I said.

"I don't believe you." Tears appeared in the corners of Sylvia's eyes.

"I think you do. Prassad is a real fucker. And Angelica is the fuckee." I should have put it more delicately, but then again Dr. Sylvia Kahn had created an entire medical specialty out of prescribing adultery. In any event, I was preoccupied with planning my getaway. I didn't want to risk running into Prassad in the waiting room. I remembered there was another door out, past the bathroom and to my right.

"Why are you telling me this, Lydia?" Sylvia was shaking now.

"Because it's even worse than that. Much worse," I said. "I need this for the record, Sylvia. Prassad wouldn't give in to Michael's terms, but he came to terms with Angelica just as soon as she inherited power of attorney. Is that correct?"

That, in the end, was what was in it for Prassad—the deal of a lifetime, the fulfillment of the New Delhi urologist's American dream. A deal that had been rapidly slipping away from him. Sylvia nodded in the affirmative, then started to sob.

I dashed behind her, past the bathroom. There was the rear fire-and-utility door that led to another door, this one opening directly onto the stairwell. I took the steps two at a time. One flight down and I was panting for air. I resolved then and there to join the McBurney Y for an entire year—if I survived this. Two flights down and Dr. Prassad Panaik stepped through the sixth-floor door with a pistol in his hand.

"I think you have a death wish, Lydia," he said.

For the first time, I had to agree with that assessment.

"Are you going to kill me? Right here?"

"If necessary," Prassad said. "But our preference is to do it back in your apartment. That would be neater, bring it all full circle. Your suicide at the scene of the crime you committed. Angelica is there as we speak, working on a draft of your suicide note, your confession. It isn't easy for her—you *are* so literary, you know."

My heart was thudding so loudly I thought there was a good chance somebody in a nearby apartment would hear it and coming running to save me. The desperate mind is a fanciful thing.

"But it looks like I'll have to kill you here and take your body there," Prassad said. He adjusted the pistol so that it was touching my chest over my heart, smack in the middle of my modest cleavage, making it a faintly sexual death threat. Pig to the end. He pushed me with the pistol against the stairwell wall.

My heart was reeling.

How many more times will you remember a certain afternoon of your childhood, some afternoon that's so deeply a part of your being that you can't even conceive of your life without it? Perhaps four or five times more. Perhaps not even . . . And yet it all seems limitless.

I kneed Prassad in the balls. Hard. The pistol dropped out of his hand and I kicked it skittering down the stairs. I ran, catching up with the gun at the next landing. One floor above me, I heard the stairwell door click shut. I grabbed the gun, raced back up the stairs, and yanked that door open. There was Dr. Prassad Panaik, pounding frantically on his wife's rear office door, begging her to unlock it and let him in.

"Fuck you!" Sylvie replied.

I wondered what Captain Amy Liu would do in a situation like this.

I smacked the back of Dr. Panaik's head with the butt of the pistol, instantly sedating him.

I met Amy at the French Roast on Eleventh Street, a coffee shop where unemployed actors and writers wait on tables that are occupied mainly by unemployed actors and writers. It gave one faith in the American economy.

As promised, Amy brought along Michael's and my Swiss bank account documents so that I, as promised, could sign the whole deal over to Paddy's ministries. While I'd been knocking out Prassad, Paddy had been making up his mind at Our Lady of Pompeii to remain in New York and to rededicate himself to saving poor souls like Manuel—to save them in Manuel's name. Knowing that he had rendered that decision while he still believed Manuel to be guilty made it easier for Paddy to meet with Manuel in his cell and guide him to the understanding that his confession had been a delusion.

"I think these belong to you also," Amy said, placing three

books on the table between us. Montaigne's *Essais,* a Baudelaire, a Zola. Antique editions all. "We found them on Mrs. Linscott's telephone table with a note to mail them to you."

"How responsible of her. For a murderess, that is."

"It was another attempt to throw a piece of suspicion in your direction, one more possible motive—to get your hands on some rare books you loved," Amy said. "In the end, their downfall was that they were too scrupulous about that. Too *much* misdirection. And way too scattered. They were trying to pin it on you, but they were grooming Bloomster as a backup if that didn't stick. Very ingenious and terribly stupid."

"So that's why they pointed me in Bloomster's direction the day after the murder?"

"And why Mrs. Linscott left Bloomster's knife in the closet, not to mention wearing his wig."

"How did she get into my apartment, by the way?"

"A key. A copy she'd made of one you lent her husband. Found it in his pocket or something."

I looked across at Amy. She seemed worn, and more than a little disheartened. "It's easy to put the story together *after* the fact, isn't it?" I said.

"That's right," Amy said. She looked me steadily in the eyes. "I have no illusions about how I performed on this case, Lydia. Not one."

"Is your offer of apology still on the table?" I said.

"Yes."

"Accepted," I said, reaching out for Amy's hand.

We shook on it, and then, like a pair of schoolgirls giddy with relief for making up after a spat, we both started to laugh.

"I really do need a friend," Amy said. "A smart one."

"Me too."

We sipped our lattes in comfortable silence.

"Barry is sleeping with a crossing guard," Amy said quietly.

"I'm sorry."

"I'm not. I haven't felt this good about myself for some time."

"Why's that?"

"Because I don't like him anymore. In fact, I haven't liked him very much for years. The man is not a pleasure to be around. At least for me. Maybe he makes the crossing guard happy."

"She probably has different expectations."

"She's probably impressed he can cross the street between the white lines."

"It's all in a woman's perspective. Not to mention her IQ. And Barry didn't strike me as within hailing distance of you in that regard."

Amy shook her head ruefully. "What gave him away?"

"His face," I said.

Amy sighed. "I loved that face once," she said. "But you want to know the God's honest truth? I think what I liked most about it was that it is so fucking un-Chinese."

"Beware of what you desire, for you will surely get it," I said.

"And then grow to hate it."

"So the crossing guard gets you off the hook?"

"That she does," Amy said. "I'm a weakling. Having a child does that to you. Makes it hard to break up a family just because your husband's touch makes your skin crawl."

"But this makes it different?"

"I guess it does. I told him to move out yesterday."

"You won't regret it, Amy."

"We'll see."

"It's funny," I said. "A couple of days ago—in my mind's eye—I saw you and Barry coming out of the Sherry-Netherland and you were looking disillusioned. Disenchanted and disillusioned." Then I told her that this image was part of what kept me from disappearing to Casablanca with Raphael.

"I would have gone with him in a heartbeat," Amy said, deadpan.

"So now you tell me," I said. We both laughed again. "How did you find out, by the way? About the crossing guard."

"I'd been suspecting it for a while," Amy said. "So one day I took the young woman for a little walk behind the school where she works. Then I beat the shit out of her until she confessed."

"Ah, the old-fashioned way." I considered a moment and then said, "Actually, I've been doing a little life reassessing myself."

"Changing careers again?"

"I've thought about it," I said. "That Learning to Love Again business certainly put me through some changes. I mean, I'm all for legalizing prostitution. But then I realized that the franchise would legalize prostitution for the rich only. Who else could afford five-hundred-dollar doctor's visits, and five-hundred-*plus* weekly surrogate sessions? Not Babycakes's clientele. So those girls would still be rounded by the vice cops. They would still get the shit beaten out of them by their non-corporate pimps and low-rent johns. "

Amy nodded in agreement. "So where does that leave you?"

"I've arranged with Paddy to put half of our newfound riches into something we call 'Working Girl Ministries.'"

"Catchy," Amy said.

"Health care and counseling. Plus a whole team of lawyers to keep them out of jail. I'm working on the incorporation papers as a nonprofit." I raised my latte mug in a toast. "At last my MBA is serving a useful purpose."

"Impressive," Amy said, clinking mugs. "But what about you? Are you staying in the trade yourself?"

"The jury's still out on that one."

About the Author

Fiona Quirina is the author of four mysteries and three medical thrillers written under her real name. Fiona's own life has some remarkable similarities to that of the fictional character, Lydia Quess. Visit her website at www.lydiaquess.com.